Cattle Valley

Gone Surfin': Like the other Cattle Valley stories this one was well worth picking up and reading. It was very enjoyable and a definite recommend read to NOR readers and to friends. The Love scenes between Quade and Kai were very sensual and sexy and made for a good and fun read
~Night Owl Romance

Gone Surfin' and Kai and Quade's story was a great edition to the Cattle Valley series ~ *Joyfully Reviewed*

The Last Bouquet: …a fabulous read with a lot of hot, steamy, and sexy love scenes…WOW!! It was well worth reading ~ *Night Owl Romance*

Carol Lynne proves that literary gay sex does not have to be rough to be exciting, and that love is a universal turn-on ~ *Author, Lisabet Sarai*

Total-E-Bound Publishing books in print from
Carol Lynne:

Campus Cravings Volume One: On the Field
Coach
Side-Lined
Sacking the Quarterback

Campus Cravings Volume Two: Off the Field
Off Season
Forbidden Freshman

Campus Cravings Volume Three: Back on Campus
Broken Pottery
In Bear's Bed

Campus Cravings Volume Four: Dorm Life
Office Advances
A Biker's Vow

Campus Cravings Volume Five: BK House
Hershie's Kiss
Theron's Return

Good-Time Boys
Sonny's Salvation
Garron's Gift
Rawley's Redemption
Twin Temptations

Cattle Valley Volume One
All Play & No Work
Cattle Valley Mistletoe

Cattle Valley Volume Two
Sweet Topping
Rough Ride

Cattle Valley Volume Three
Physical Therapy
Out of the Shadow

Cattle Valley Volume Four
Bad Boy Cowboy
The Sound of White

Poker Night
Texas Hold 'em
Slow-Play

CATTLE VALLEY
Volume Five

Gone Surfin'

The Last Bouquet

CAROL LYNNE

Cattle Valley: Volume Five
ISBN # 978-1-907010-90-3
©Copyright Carol Lynne 2009
Cover Art by April Martinez ©Copyright 2009
Interior text design by Claire Siemaszkiewicz
Total-E-Bound Publishing

GONE SURFIN'

Dedication

For the members of my yahoo group who
continually push me for more, I thank you.

Chapter One

"Just deal with it!" Quade yelled, burying his face in his hands. He heard a shuffling noise before Hurricane Carol hit the room.

"What the heck are you getting paid for again? Because I seem to recall your paycheque being a hell of a lot more than mine."

"Drop it, Carol. Just type up an email cancelling the damn Christmas Party and send it out."

"Well, Merry Christmas to you too, Mr. Scrooge."

Quade glanced up from his hands to stare at the pain in his ass. At five-feet two-inches, Carol was worse than any haemorrhoid on the planet. "I'm busy trying to get the roads cleared in time for Christmas."

Carol got that look on her face that Quade hated. "Where's your shovel? I don't see any shovel. If you don't have a shovel, then you aren't doing shit about snow removal. Which means, Mr. Scrooge, that you have time to send out a damn email!"

Quade threw up his hands and shook his head. "Seriously. I know you enjoy this witty banter of yours, but I'm really not in the mood to step into the ring with you. At least not right now. I'll pencil this discussion in for next Tuesday. How does that sound?"

Carol crossed her arms and slumped into the chair in front of Quade's desk. "Kai still hasn't returned your call, has he?"

Despite being his nemesis, Carol was also his best friend. "Yes. As a matter of fact, Kai called a few hours ago. He just finished competing for the season and wanted me to join him in Oahu for the holidays. But I can't, because Mother Nature decided to fuck with me."

"Bummer," Carol echoed Quade's thoughts.

"Yeah. So forgive me if I'm not in the best of moods."

With a resigned sigh, Carol stood. "So tell me what I should say in this very important email."

Quade rolled his eyes and sat back in his chair. "I don't know. Due to the fact that it's colder than a witch's tit in a brass brazier, that the roads are piled with more snow than we've seen in a half-century, the annual Christmas in the Park and Party will be cancelled."

Carol pursed her lips in disapproval. "I think I can come up with something a little more tactful than that."

"See? You didn't need my help after all."

Without another word, Carol turned and strode from his office, slamming the door on her way out. "Good riddance," Quade fumed.

No sooner had he wiped the episode with his secretary from his mind, than the phone rang. "Crap. What now?" Quade reached across his desk and picked up the handset. "Quade," he answered.

"Hey," Sheriff Blackfeather replied. "I was wondering if you'd take a short ride with me."

"Is this a date?" Quade quipped. "Because I'm not sure if I'm up to defending my life against those two hoodlums you call partners."

"Not in the mood," Ryan Blackfeather admonished.

"Fine. So tell me why we're going for a ride?"

"I need your superb math skills to help me figure out the salt situation at the City Barn."

"Sure, flattery works every time. Give me time to jump into my Michelin Man suit, and I'll meet you out front." Quade hung up and dug his snowsuit out of the small closet in his office. After taking off his house slippers, he climbed into the puffy white suit.

"I'm heading to the City Barn with Ryan," he told Carol as he exited his office. He went to grab his boots and stopped. "Um, did a burglar break in, or have you done something with my boots?"

Carol glanced at him over the top of her reading glasses. "What? You can't wear your slippers?"

"Hey. Don't knock the slippers. Now, where are my boots?"

Carol pointed across the room to the heating vent. "Thought maybe dry footwear would put you in a better mood."

Quade gave his friend a grunt. "Sorry to disappoint. Unless the sun came out, the temperature rose to eighty-five and palm trees sprouted up through the ground, I'm gonna be grouchy."

He used the chair in front of Carol's desk to sit and lace up his boots. He knew he was being a royal ass, but his heart felt like it was breaking. For the first time in years he had someone who actually wanted to spend the holidays with him, but his duty as mayor wouldn't let him enjoy it.

"Maybe when all of this is over," Carol tried to soothe.

"By the time this is over, Kai'll be getting ready to go back on tour," he pouted.

Standing, he went back to the heater and retrieved his gloves. "I shouldn't be gone long."

"I'll alert the media," Carol replied in a deadpan monotone.

Still shaking his head, Quade walked out of the building. Ryan's SUV was idling at the bottom of the courthouse steps. Quade quickly got in and slammed the door. "Hey," he greeted.

Ryan covered a yawn and nodded his hello. When Ryan didn't make a move to drive off, Quade threw up his hands. "Anytime."

Ryan pointed towards the unused seatbelt over Quade's shoulder. "Come on," Quade whined. "That thing'll strangle me in this getup."

Ryan shook his head. "Better to be strangled than thrown through a windshield."

With a growl of annoyance, Quade fastened the safety belt. "Happy?"

"No. What would make me happy is being home playing in front of the fire with the men I love," Ryan barked.

Quade grinned. "Glad to see I'm not the only one pissed at Mother Nature."

"The bitch," Ryan grumbled, pulling away from the curb.

"So, what am I calculating?" Quade asked.

"Our salt supply is dwindling at an alarming rate. I need someone to figure out if we have enough to plough and then salt the road up to the lodge. I'm afraid if we don't, the packed snow and ice will be there until spring. Dealing with dead tourists is not the way I care to spend my winter."

"Okay, but don't we have an engineer on staff to figure this shit out?" *God,* did he have to do *everyone's* job?

"Yes, that would be Ed, but he's home puking his guts up. Besides, last time I checked, you were also an engineer."

"A non-practicing engineer," Quade added.

"You're still better than anything else I've got."

"Gee, thanks."

Ryan came to a stop outside the large structure used to house the salt and sand mixture as well as the other city equipment. Bracing himself for the blast of frigid air, Quade turned to Ryan. "Let's get this over with."

* * * *

Stepping out of his snow gear, Quade walked through his living room to the kitchen. He went straight to the coffee pot and made a fresh batch. Waiting for the coffee to brew, he looked out the set of French doors to the tarp-covered pool. "I miss you," he crooned to the lonely pit of cement. At least he was happy to see his state-of-the-art heated cover had done its job. No telling what kind of damage the pool would've sustained had the snow been allowed to accumulate on the cover.

The beeping of the coffee pot pulled him away from the view. He grabbed his cup from the sink where he'd set it that morning and poured the elixir of the gods into it. Mug in hand, Quade moved to his favourite chair and settled in. He looked at the gas fireplace across from him and moaned. The remote was on the mantel. Damn.

Too tired to get up, he threw the blanket from the back of his chair over his lap and picked up the television remote. A show on the Travel Channel caught his attention. With his thumb hovering over the channel button, Quade argued with himself. *You know you'll just get more depressed if you watch this. Turn it to something else. No. If I can't see Hawaii first hand, at least I can watch others having fun in the sun.*

He took a sip of his coffee and fixated on the surfers in the background. *Maybe Kai's out there?* A commercial came on, ruining the moment. Quade's thumb finally connected with the channel button as he moved on.

After an hour of watching Sponge Bob, he turned off the television and picked up the book on the table beside him. When he opened the mystery to where he'd left off, a bookmark fell to his lap. Quade picked up the snapshot of Kai.

Gazing at the gorgeous man, Quade moaned. Why did he continue to do this to himself? It had been ten months since he'd said goodbye to the younger man. Despite the phone call earlier, Quade had no doubt Kai had been filling his time with all sorts of surfing groupies. A man that hot couldn't be expected to be faithful. Hell, they hadn't even mentioned the L word.

Quade knew he had no hold on Kai. Maybe things would've turned out differently if he'd been honest and professed his feelings? Naw. He'd have just ended up with egg on his face.

Maybe he should put up a tree? He hadn't had a Christmas tree in years, but he knew there was a small four-footer in the attic. Replacing the photo between the pages, Quade tossed the book aside and stood. "No time like the present," his voice echoed through the empty room.

* * * *

Still in his robe, Quade stared at the shabby tree. *I really should take it down.* After several minutes of arguing with himself, he decided to wait until the next day. Yep, New Year's Day is the perfect time to clean. There wasn't anything else going on except a town full of people trying to survive hangovers from the previous night's festivities.

As usual, his Christmas had sucked. Spending Christmas with his family back in Charleston wasn't an option. It had been years since he'd been to his parents' house. Quade knew his friends thought the estrangement had been brought on by his homosexuality, but the truth was, he'd simply never liked Nelson and Lorraine Madison. He'd spent his entire childhood trying to live up to the family name. Until, at the age of twenty-six, he'd realised being a Madison of the Charleston Madison's wasn't all it was cracked up to be.

He'd ended up going over to Carol's house for Christmas dinner just to shut the woman up. The only bright spot of the entire day was the brief phone call he'd received from Kai.

His lover had told him he missed him, and things weren't going well with his career. Quade already knew Kai had dropped dramatically in the standings the previous year. He'd tried his best to give the younger man encouragement for the upcoming season, telling Kai he could do anything he set his mind to.

The words Quade had longed to say to his lover sat on the tip of his tongue but didn't budge. He once again vowed not to show his hand until they were together again. Quade knew he'd be able to tell when he saw Kai. The man's soulful brown eyes were easy to read.

He looked at the wall calendar. Only thirty-seven days until his annual vacation. Maybe he should call the travel agent and see if he could move his departure up by thirty-six days. Quade sighed. Knowing his luck, he'd try and surprise his lover only to find Kai in bed with someone else. *Surprise!*

Yawning, Quade stretched and rubbed his stomach through his thick terrycloth robe. Maybe a nap was in order? If he was lucky, maybe he'd sleep right through the big party and wake just in time to catch his plane for Hawaii.

Chuckling, Quade shuffled to the bedroom. A guy could hope, couldn't he?

Chapter Two

Arriving at the big New Year's Eve party, Quade immediately noticed Ryan and his men. Instead of doing the usual hobnobbing, the threesome seemed lost in their own world of giggles and sly touches. *How depressing.*

Detouring towards the bar, Quade ordered bourbon and scanned the room. Drink in hand, he tugged on his shirt collar. Damn he hated suits, especially tuxedos. He spotted a mountain of a man coming towards him and grinned. "Hey."

"Hey yourself," Ezra grumbled.

Quade looked around Ezra's incredible bulk. "Where's your better half?"

Ezra shrugged. "Gossiping, no doubt."

"That can't be. I just saw Nate occupied with Ryan and Rio." The two men looked at each other and laughed. It was well known around town that Nate had the scoop on everyone in the community. Quade still didn't understand how the man managed to have so many friends. Hell, Nate had more friends than he did and he'd lived in Cattle Valley five times longer.

"No," Ezra's laugh died to a chuckle. "He's talking to Richard and Chad."

Quade nodded and took another sip of his drink. "The place looks fantastic," Quade commented, looking around at the ballroom. "When am I gonna get a tour of The Grizzly Bar?"

"Now if you want one," Ezra offered.

Out of his peripheral vision, Quade saw George Manning coming towards him. Shit. He knew the fire captain would want to discuss city budgets again. The man thought of nothing else besides work.

"Let's go," Quade declared, and took off for the bar.

Evidently, Ezra knew exactly why Quade practically ran to the opposite end of the lodge. "That bad, huh?"

Quade glanced over his shoulder. "You have no idea. Don't get me wrong. I like George, but the man is a pain in the ass. He needs to learn to loosen up once in a while."

The large heavily carved doors of The Grizzly Bar were propped open and Quade noticed several people milling around. "Is it open for business?" he asked, looking down at his empty glass.

"Not officially, but I'm sure I can hook you up. We decided to let people get a first look at the bar during the party."

Ezra took Quade's glass out of his hand and moved towards the bar. "What were you drinkin'?"

"Bourbon," Quade answered. The room was spectacular. "You've done a great job. I can see why Brewster was desperate enough to hire someone to delay the opening."

Ezra handed his drink over and gazed around the room. "I'd love to take the credit, but it was all Wyn and Richard. They wanted the rustic cabin feel."

"Well, they got it in spades." Quade could easily picture himself sitting beside the fire with Kai wrapped around him. Thinking of Kai started him on a downhill slide. He thought about the phone in his pocket. "Would you excuse me for a minute? I need to make a call."

"Sure. I'll go find my wayward partner. Hopefully dinner will be served soon. I'm starving."

"Save me a place at your table," Quade called out. "If I'm stuck with Ryan and his playmates, I might just slit my wrists."

Laughing, Ezra acknowledged the request with a nod of his head.

Alone, Quade pulled out his phone and called Kai. He'd tried earlier in the day, but Kai must've had his phone off because it went straight to voicemail. Quade refused to wonder why his lover never returned the call.

"Hello," Kai's smooth voice answered.

"Hey. It's me."

"Quade," Kai sounded surprised.

Quade heard shuffling in the background before Kai's voice came back on. "How're you doing?"

"Fine," Quade answered. "I thought I'd call and wish you a happy New Year."

"Uh, thanks. Listen, I hate to cut you off, but I'm headed for a big party, and I'm not near ready. Can I talk to you later?"

The dismissal hurt, but Quade refused to let Kai hear it in his voice. "Sure. I'll be around."

"I'm glad you called."

"Yeah," Quade managed to get out. "Later." Quade closed the phone and stuck it back into his pocket. Shit. Now he felt worse than before.

He quickly finished off his drink before heading towards the ballroom. Maybe a nice dinner would get his mind off his broken heart.

* * * *

Kai gave himself one last glance in the full-length mirror. For a rental, the tux fit surprisingly well. He cupped his hand over his mouth to check his breath once again. Still minty fresh. Excellent. He planned to do a lot of kissing in the hours to come.

He stepped out of the dressing room, clothes he'd worn into the store, tucked under his arm and walked towards the counter. "Fits perfectly. I hope you don't mind if I wear it out? I'm already late for a party at the new lodge in Cattle Valley."

The clerk behind the counter shrugged. "As long as you're paying, I don't care what you do."

After settling his bill, Kai left the shop. He unlocked the backdoor on the SUV and threw his wrinkled clothes inside. He hoped the nap he'd managed to squeeze in on the plane would be enough to get him through the evening. With a little luck, he'd be up well into the wee hours of the morning.

Getting behind the wheel, Kai checked the map once more. The nice lady at the rental car agency had told him the roads were in abhorrent condition and would be even worse the further south he drove. She'd suggested a four-wheel drive to ensure his safety and Kai had taken her advice.

It took him longer than he anticipated to get to the small town he'd heard so much about, and Kai began to worry he'd miss dinner. The quick burger he'd managed to grab between flights in LA hadn't stayed with him long. He could've eaten in Sheridan, but his nerves refused to entertain the thought. What he was truly hungry for he knew he wouldn't find on any café menu.

After probably the scariest drive in his life, Kai arrived at the Tall Pines Lodge. It took him several moments of sitting in the SUV to get his heart rate back under control. Snow was definitely not his thing. He'd grown up in Hawaii for God's sake. What was he supposed to know about slick roads and snow drifts?

He looked through the windshield at the building in front of him. *What if Quade brought a date?* Shit. He hadn't really considered that possibility, but the more he thought about it, the more sense it made. For the fifth time in an hour, Kai kicked himself for the brush-off he'd given the man earlier. Surely Quade wouldn't have called him if he was on a date?

With that in mind, Kai walked up the hotel steps. The moment of truth, he thought as he stood in the ballroom doorway. He spotted Quade right away, his gaze zooming in on the man he'd dreamed about incessantly.

Quade's eyes locked with his, and Kai knew his lover was surprised when he began to choke. Some guy beside him started pounding Quade on the back. Kai's feet were frozen to the floor, wondering if the well-groomed man was Quade's date. He let out a sigh of relief when Quade stood and strode towards him.

The hungry look on Quade's face put the rest of Kai's nerves to rest. Yes! He felt like shouting. In a matter of seconds, Quade's soft lips were pressed to his own. Kai wrapped his arms around his lover and took the kiss deeper, needing more reassurance than he was prepared to acknowledge.

At that point, Kai couldn't have cared less what the rest of the people in the room thought of them. He ate Quade's mouth like the starving man he was. A soft whimper escaped him as Quade finally broke the kiss.

"I can't believe you're here, right in front of me," Quade said.

"I'm sorry," Kai apologised. "I just couldn't stay away any longer."

Quade shook his head vehemently. "Don't apologise. If you knew how much I've missed you…"

"I hope I'm not barging in on a date or anything," Kai interrupted.

"Date?" Quade chuckled. "I haven't even entertained the thought of going out with anyone else since I left Hawaii."

Quade's face took on a concerned look. "What about you? I mean, I know I don't have the right to ask, but…are you dating anyone else?"

Kai shook his head. How could Quade think such a thing? In the short time they'd had together, Quade had shown him what it was like being with a real man, one who didn't let his eyes roam to other men when they were out together, a guy who was actually still in his bed come morning.

"No one could compete with you," Kai finally answered. "You've got my head so screwed up that I couldn't even concentrate on surfing."

Kai knew in his heart it was one of the main reasons he'd come to Wyoming. With his surfing career on the line, he had to find out whether or not his feelings were real. Gazing into Quade's green eyes, he had a strong sense they were.

His stomach chose that moment to growl, making Quade chuckle. "Hungry?" he asked, rubbing Kai's stomach.

God he wanted to move that hand further south. "You have no idea."

"Come on," Quade said, wrapping an arm around Kai's waist. "Let's see if Chad can scrounge you up another plate."

Kai's steps faltered when Quade started to lead him to the table. "I don't want to impose on your friends."

"Don't worry about them. Hell, they'll probably welcome you with open arms." Quade winced. "I've been a tad grouchy lately."

"Really? You?" Kai was genuinely surprised. He'd never known Quade to be anything but easy going.

Stopping next to the table, Quade introduced him. "Ezra, Wyn, this is Kai Hachiya."

The man Quade introduced as Ezra stood and held out his hand. Holy shit. Kai had never seen a hand so big. He met the man halfway and shook his hand. "Nice to meet you," Kai greeted.

Ezra was unceremoniously pulled back before the much smaller man took his place. "It's so nice to finally meet you. I've seen your picture a number of times, but it definitely didn't do you justice."

Kai looked from Wyn over his shoulder to Quade. "Picture?"

Quade's face turned a pretty shade of red. "Uh, yeah, I've got a picture of you on my desk. Wyn's forever dropping by to bother me about something."

The thought of Quade having his picture out for anyone to see, warmed Kai. He turned and gave Quade a peck on the lips. "Thank you," he whispered.

"For what?" Quade asked.

"For not forgetting me," Kai answered.

"Not remotely possible," Quade declared.

Quade pulled out a chair. "Have a seat, and I'll go find you something to eat. What'll you have to drink?" Quade asked, before rushing off.

"Just water."

Quade's eyes glanced at the full glass of liquor on the table. "Maybe I should switch to water as well."

Kai shrugged. "I don't care if you drink."

Quade bent down and spoke into Kai's ear. "I have better things planned than passing out before midnight."

"Glad we're on the same page," Kai whispered.

He stared at Quade's back as his lover made his way through the crowded room. Quade was definitely giving Daniel Craig a run for his money in that tux.

"So," Wyn interrupted Kai's thoughts. "How long are you planning to stay?"

"I'm not really sure," Kai answered. "I don't have much going on until I leave for Australia in mid-February."

"Quade's booked on a flight the first week in February to go back to Hawaii," Wyn commented.

Kai already knew that, but how did these people? He wasn't sure he'd like the idea of everyone knowing his business. Growing up in Honolulu, the small town life-style was totally foreign to him.

Trying to be polite to Quade's friends, Kai nodded. "I'll probably wait and follow him back to Oahu."

"Have you given any thought to becoming a land-lover?"

"Wyn!" Ezra admonished. "Don't scare the man off." Ezra gave Kai an apologetic grin. "Wyn likes to fancy himself the town den mother."

Wyn smiled and slapped the giant man on the shoulder. "I'm curious. So sue me."

Kai didn't know what to say, so he simply sat in silence until Quade returned carrying a large plate of food. "I wasn't sure what you were hungry for, so I got you a little of everything," Quade informed him, setting the plate on the table.

"Thanks." Without preamble, Kai dug into his food. He wanted to get the eating out of the way so he could go back to kissing.

"Would you be interested in going back to my house when you're done?" Quade asked, putting his hand on Kai's thigh.

"Sure, but what about your friends?"

"They can go to their own houses. Mine only has room for the two of us," Quade joked.

Kai smiled. He'd missed Quade's sense of humour. "Will you get into trouble for not ringing in the New Year here?"

"No," Quade squeezed Kai's inner thigh. "And even if I did, do I look as if I'd care?" Quade's hand continued to travel upward until several of his fingers flitted across the bulge in Kai's pants.

Dropping his fork on his plate, Kai wiped his mouth with a napkin. "I've had enough food. Let's go."

Chapter Three

Kai stood on the porch of The Tall Pines with Quade's hand in his. "Wouldn't you just rather stay here?"

Quade's head tilted to the side. "Are you serious?"

The thought of risking his life again on the narrow winding mountain roads caused bile to rise in his throat. "I don't think I can drive down. God help me, I don't know how you people drive around in this crap, but my hands are still cramped from the white-knuckle trip up."

Chuckling, Quade lifted Kai's hand and kissed it. "I'll get you down. We'll figure out how to get your rental later."

"What if I barf?"

Quade started down the steps, pulling Kai behind him. "Then you'll clean it up. Just relax."

"Easy for you to say." He gripped Quade's hand like a life-line until his lover opened the passenger door to a huge white Escalade. "Nice ride," he commented.

"Thanks. Give me your keys, and I'll get your bags out of your rental."

Kai handed over the key ring. "I could've done it. I'm so freaked I didn't even think about clothes."

"Good. Let's keep it that way," Quade slid in.

Quade shut the passenger door and turned to the line of vehicles. Kai was sure it wasn't hard for Quade to pick out the rental, surely knew everyone in town and what they drove. Walking over to the SUV, Kai watched as Quade hit the automatic door lock on the key fob. After a quick glance at the front seat, Quade shut the door and went around back. Kai was slightly embarrassed when Quade began picking up his loose clothing and stuffing them into the large blue duffle. Had he known Quade would be the one handling his bag, Kai would've packed his dirty clothes back inside.

Quade walked back to the Escalade with a smile plastered to his face. He stowed the duffle in the back of his SUV and got in behind the wheel. Before pulling out of the parking lot, he leaned across the console. "Give me a kiss."

Kai was happy to oblige. Not only had he missed the taste of his lover, but a kiss would definitely stall the ride down. Maybe if he got Quade horny enough, his lover would agree to stay at the lodge instead of risking life and limb.

He took the kiss deeper, reaching over to the fly of Quade's tuxedo pants. As he ran his fingers over the soft material, the bulge in the older man's lap began to grow. Kai smiled to himself as he sucked on Quade's tongue.

Quade must have seen the slight smirk on his face, because he pulled back and studied Kai. "Darlin', as good as that feels I'm still driving down this mountain. If you'd rather I do it with my mind on my cock instead of the road, so be it."

Kai's hand stilled in the process of unzipping his lover's fly. "Why's it so important we drive down now?"

Quade pressed Kai's hand against his arousal once more before releasing it. "Because I've fantasised about you in my bed for damn near a year. It's New Year's Eve and I'd like to ring in the occasion with my cock buried in your ass. Is that reason enough?"

Removing his hand, Kai rubbed his own hard-on. "Drive, just…just be careful."

He received a playful kiss before Quade put the SUV into gear. "Of course I will. I'm carrying precious cargo."

* * * *

Quade was still chuckling as he pulled into his garage. Kai had ridden the imaginary break on the passenger's side the entire trip. Turning off the engine, Quade leaned over and pried Kai's graceful fingers from the dash. "We're here. You can relax now."

"I may never relax again," Kai choked.

Feeling slightly guilty, Quade extricated himself from the Escalade and went around to the passenger's side. Opening Kai's door, he helped the younger man out of the vehicle. "Let's get you inside and in front of a fire."

"Throw in a stiff drink and you've got yourself a deal."

Smiling, Quade led Kai into the house. He switched on the kitchen light, and turned to his lover. He hated to admit that he didn't even know what kind of liquor the man preferred. "What can I get you? I have beer, bourbon, wine and probably some vodka in the freezer."

"Beer."

With a nod, Quade released his hold on Kai's waist and opened the refrigerator. Deciding he'd had enough bourbon for one night, Quade fished out two cans, handing one to Kai.

"Thanks," Kai said, taking the can. "Is it cold in here, or is it just me?"

Beer in hand, Quade went to check on the thermostat. "Seventy-one, but I'll turn it up until we go to bed. Nothing's worse than trying to sleep under the covers if the house is too warm."

Quade knew there would be some adjustments he'd have to make to accommodate Kai's sudden visit, and he was more than willing to do them. He still couldn't believe the man he'd fantasised about for so long was standing in his kitchen. "Why don't we go into the living room, and I'll turn on the fire."

"Great house," Kai commented on their way to the living room.

"Thanks. I had it built after the first year I moved here." Quade turned to Kai and slipped the light jacket from his shoulders. "We'll have to get you a warmer coat."

Quade had a closet full of coats, but he knew all of them would be too big for Kai. After hanging up their coats in the closet, he turned back towards the man he'd fallen for all those months ago. Kai definitely hadn't changed in appearance. The man was still the most gorgeous surfer on the professional circuit. "You cut your hair," Quade observed.

Kai's long fingers threaded through the short dark brown locks. "Yeah," Kai bit off.

The way his lover said it, Quade could tell it was a touchy subject. The last thing he wanted was to make Kai uncomfortable. Quade gestured to the deep sofa. "Have a seat, and I'll get us another beer."

"Sounds good," Kai answered, taking off his tuxedo jacket, tie and vest. "You don't mind if I get comfortable, do you?"

"Not at all. I'll get your bag out of the SUV while I'm at it." Quade started for the kitchen, but stopped and looked over his shoulder at Kai. "Uh, just because I'm getting your luggage doesn't mean I want you to put clothes on."

Kai chuckled for the first time. Hopefully the anxiety caused by the ride down the mountain was starting to wear off. "Is that an invitation to get naked?"

"No invitation needed. I'm all about nudity when I'm home." Quade gave Kai a wink before leaving the room. He retrieved the duffle from the back of the Escalade and set it on the kitchen table. Quade noticed his hands were sweaty and wiped them on a dishtowel. *Why do I feel so nervous? I finally have the man of my dreams in my damn living room.* "Straighten the fuck up," he scolded himself.

While he was in the kitchen, Quade shrugged out of his jacket, tie and vest. At least he knew Kai had stripped down that far. He would've gladly stripped naked, but didn't want to assume anything too early in their reunion. A vision of Kai rubbing his cock in the car came to mind, and Quade immediately went hard. Yeah, hopefully they had the same game plan.

Stopping at the fridge to get another couple of beers, Quade strolled to the living room. Kai sat in a ball on the sofa with a blanket wrapped around him. If Quade wasn't mistaken, his lover's teeth were chattering. He wanted to laugh at the sun-worshipping god he'd found on the beach. Quade doubted Kai would acclimate to the cold weather anytime soon.

He went to stand in front of the couch and noticed a pile of black and white clothing on the floor. *Woo hoo.* They definitely had the same game plan. "Comfortable?" he asked, setting their beer down on the table.

"Cold," Kai managed around chattering teeth.

"I'd like to apply for the job as your personal furnace," Quade said smoothly. He unbuttoned his shirt, maintaining eye contact with the younger man.

Kai grinned and opened the blanket, spreading his thighs at the same time. The first look of Kai in all his bronzed glory in eleven months almost sent Quade to his knees. "Fuck, you're beautiful," he ground out.

Kai's long thin cock was semi-hard and resting on his flat stomach. Quade licked his lips as he unfastened his pants and let them fall to the floor. "You've waxed recently," he commented, giving in to his body's demands and dropping to the floor.

Chuckling, Kai nodded and cupped Quade's cheek. "Do you remember the swim trunks I like to wear?"

Quade closed his eyes and thought about the first day he'd spotted Kai on Waikiki Beach. The gorgeous man had been surrounded by both men and women. Quade had had to flip to his stomach to avoid public embarrassment.

The tiny red bikini bottoms were enough to make a grown man cry. Quade didn't dare approach the god signing autographs. He wasn't sure who he was, but the younger man deserved all the praise he got.

"I remember drooling so much the first day I saw you that there was a wet spot in the sand below my chin," Quade joked.

Quade opened his eyes and stared at Kai. "I still can't believe you brushed off all those people to come over and introduce yourself."

"How could I not? A hot guy was eating me alive with his eyes. Of course I wanted to take advantage of the situation."

Quade decided to ask the question he'd been stewing over since. "But why me? Surely you have hundreds of men ogling that fine ass of yours. Why approach a middle-aged man with a quickly receding hairline?"

Kai reached out and ran his hands down Quade's nude back to land on his ass. "I'm not the only one with a fine ass."

When Quade started to shake his head in denial, Kai continued. "It was an immediate attraction that I still can't explain. All I know is I glanced over and there you were, and I was hooked."

Deciding not to look a gift horse in the mouth, Quade bent and nuzzled Kai's balls with his nose, licking the soft skin just under the firm sac. Kai groaned and scooted further down on the sofa, giving Quade better access.

God he'd missed the smell and taste of his lover. Quade didn't know how long the younger man would remain interested in him, but he was sure as hell going to take advantage of the time he'd been gifted.

He let his tongue roam the thin skin of Kai's perineum as he wrapped a fist around his lover's cock.

"Oh," Kai moaned. "Missed you. Missed this."

Quade looked up the length of Kai's body. The question of Kai's fidelity was forefront in his mind, but he couldn't bring himself to ask. He'd never been in a monogamous relationship, so how in the world could he expect to have one with a guy he hadn't seen in eleven months.

Knowing he had the beginnings of a five o'clock shadow, Quade ran his chin lightly over Kai's puckered hole.

"Oh yes, that, do that again," Kai panted, hooking his arms under his knees and pulling his thighs against his body.

Quade obliged his lover and ground his chin against Kai's hole, before sliding his tongue against the abraded skin to soothe. "Shall we take this into the bedroom?"

Kai nodded and Quade started to help the younger man to his feet. "Shit," Quade spat. "I didn't know you were coming. Please tell me you brought stuff?"

Chuckling, Kai nodded again. "In my bag."

Quade untangled his dress pants from around his ankles and kicked off his shoes. After making a detour to the kitchen to grab Kai's duffle, Quade led his lover into the master bedroom.

Quade pulled the down-comforter to the foot of the bed as he scrambled to get his black socks off. Kai wasted no time jumping to the centre of the California king mattress. "All kinds of room to play," Kai mused.

Tossing Kai's bag on the bed, Quade retrieved the bottle of lube from his bedside drawer. With a noise that could only be described as a giggle, Kai sat on his knees and unzipped the duffle. "Ta da!" Kai exclaimed, holding up the large box of condoms.

The look of discovery on Kai's face made him look like a boy at Christmas. Quade wasn't exactly sure how old Kai was, but he'd guess in his early twenties. God he hoped he was at least in his twenties. "How old are you?" he asked before he could think better of it.

Kai's face took on a look of surprise. "Twenty-six. Why?"

Quade shook his head and positioned himself between Kai's thighs, knocking the duffle to the floor. "Just wondering how big a pervert I really am," he commented.

Kai took the bottle of lube out of Quade's hand, getting his attention. "Is that what this is about? You into young men?"

"Hell no," Quade answered. "I'm into *you*. I guess I never realised I was twelve years your senior."

"Is that a problem?" Kai asked.

Quade didn't know whether to be honest or not. "Not now, but it could become one down the line."

He couldn't help but notice the dimming light in his lover's eyes. *Shit.* Quade tossed the lube to the mattress and wrapped his arms around Kai. "I'm sorry. I just need to be real with myself before I get in too deep. You've got your whole life in front of you, and I'm quickly approaching the downhill slide."

Kai pushed against Quade's chest. "What're you saying? You think because I'm young I don't know how I feel?"

That definitely wasn't the response Quade was expecting. Did Kai have genuine feelings for him? "I don't know how you feel. All I know is that I'm falling more in love with you every day. I tried to play it off as a vacation fling, but I haven't been able to get you off my mind since the day you drove me to the airport. I've been absolutely miserable without you."

"Well so have I," Kai interrupted. "Did you even bother to notice the way my standings continued to plummet as the season went on? You're all I think about. I may be young, but I sure as hell know what love is."

"My hair's starting to fall out," Quade reminded Kai.

"Yeah it is," Kai agreed. "Luckily I'm not in love with your hair."

Quade needed to put the brakes on this particular discussion before he made a complete fool of himself. He knew Kai meant what he said, but the man was also too young to make a lifelong decision.

Glancing at the clock, Quade saw that he had an hour to make things right between them. He couldn't bring himself to start the new year off on anything but a positive foot.

Chapter Four

Kai studied Quade as his lover seemed to take a mental time out. He couldn't believe Quade was making such an issue of twelve fucking years. There had to be more to it than that.

Maybe in time Quade would learn to trust him enough to be honest, because Kai didn't plan on going anywhere until he got his mind back on track. He'd followed his family's wishes and stayed in Oahu for Christmas, but that particular holiday was over.

As soon as Kai could arrange a flight, he'd taken off in search of answers. He'd had flings in the past, hell, tons of them if he were honest, but none of them left the aching impression the last one had. There was something about Quade that Kai couldn't seem to shake.

Quade's weather roughened hand ran down Kai's chest. "I'm glad you're here," Quade whispered, looking down at Kai.

"Really? Cuz I was starting to feel like a pimple-faced kid running after you."

The corner of Quade's lip curled into a rakish grin. "No need to run. I'm right here."

Kai shook his head. Did the man have any idea how sexy he was? He reached up and clasped his hands around the back of Quade's neck. "Come down here and kiss me."

Quade, once again, insinuated himself between Kai's spread thighs. He started to lean down for the kiss, but stopped and gazed into Kai's eyes. "I love you," Quade declared.

The words warmed Kai from the inside out. The expression on Quade's face told him the man was sincere in the declaration, so why all the baggage? Maybe Quade had been burned by a younger man in his past?

Kai decided to prove to his lover he was mature enough to handle a committed relationship. Closing the distance, Kai initiated the kiss he'd practically begged for earlier. He swept his tongue around the interior of Quade's mouth, groaning as he felt the evidence of his lover's renewed lust.

As the kiss became almost feral, he felt Quade reach for the dropped bottle of lube. Maybe this was the only thing that worked right between them for now, but he was determined to ease himself into every facet of Quade's life. He'd make it so the man couldn't imagine living without him.

With a new plan in place, Kai wrapped his legs around Quade's torso. "Fuck me." He heard the click in the quiet room as Quade opened the bottle of lubricant.

"I was hoping to be inside you at the stroke of midnight. If I fuck you now, I won't be much good to you when the new year rolls around."

Kai heard the subtle insecurity creeping into Quade's voice. Glancing over at the clock, Kai reached out and yanked the chord from the wall. The clock dimmed, but continued to stay lit. "What the fuck?"

Quade chuckled. "Batteries. When you live in a town that often loses power, you go for the battery backup."

Huffing in exasperation, Kai threw the offending gadget across the room. "Now, we can celebrate the new year on our own time schedule."

He pulled Quade's head down for another deep kiss. "Happy New Year," he whispered.

Grinning, Quade placed his lubed fingers at Kai's hole. "Let's make it three minutes 'til. That way I can be in you when the imaginary clock strikes."

Kai gasped as Quade began stretching his hole. "Am I hurting you?" Quade asked, concern written in every line of the lovely man's face.

"No, keep going. It's just been awhile." He'd already told Quade he hadn't been dating, but truth was he couldn't even pleasure himself lately. Every touch he tried to bestow on his most intimate body parts left him feeling even more depressed.

Slowly, Quade continued to insert digits, peppering Kai's face and neck with kisses the entire time. "Think you're ready?" Quade asked.

"Beyond ready," Kai panted, reaching down to rub his erection.

When Quade pulled his fingers out to sit back on his heels, Kai felt suddenly lost. "Need you," he pouted.

"Hold on, babe. I've got to get suited up," Quade chuckled.

Kai watched Quade rip the foil packet open with his teeth before rolling the condom down that big fat dick he loved so much. How many dreams had he had about Quade's beautiful cock?

Before he knew it, Quade was back in his arms. "How do you want me?" Kai inquired.

"Every way I can get you, but for now, stay where you are," Quade commanded, guiding the head of his cock through the outer ring of muscles.

Kai took several deep breaths and pushed out to make his lover's entry easier for both of them. The burning sensation hit him first. Yes. God, he'd missed this. Once the crown was in, Quade rocked back and forth, easing his entire length inside.

"Yesss," Kai hissed. Within moments the burn was replaced with ecstasy. He lifted his hips to meet Quade's slow, deliberate thrusts. "Is it New Year yet?" he asked, opening one eye to stare at Quade.

"Not yet," Quade informed him.

Kai pulled Quade down fully on top of him, his cock trapped between them. The delicious feel of Quade's stomach rubbing against his erection threatened to spoil their festivities. "Better hurry or you'll be celebrating alone," he warned Quade.

Manoeuvring his arms under Kai's knees, Quade nearly split him in two in an attempt to plunge deeper. Kai welcomed the new position, groaning loudly as his lover's cock rubbed and prodded against his prostate. He felt his balls tighten. "Can't hold it much longer," he informed Quade.

"Yeah. Yeah," Quade panted, pistoning his cock hard and deep.

The erratic thrusts were the first sign Quade was losing his control. "Do it," Kai prodded. Tears welled in his eyes with the effort it took to stave off his orgasm.

"Happy New Year, love," Quade shouted, burying himself as deep as possible inside Kai.

Kai let himself go, feeling the climax wash over him in a tidal wave. He actually struggled to breathe as his cock continued to shoot seed between them. "Fuck!" he gasped, when air finally returned to his lungs.

The mind blowing orgasm left Kai completely limp. Had he ever come that hard? He knew the answer was definitely not. There was something about Quade and Kai's feelings for the man that created an unbelievable combination.

He licked his dry lips as Quade released his legs. "I may never walk again," Kai confessed.

Quade chuckled, and rolled to the side. "Good to know I haven't lost my touch," Quade boasted.

"You still got it, Kahuna," Kai said, calling Quade the name of the Hawaiian god of sun, sand and surf.

* * * *

The following Monday morning, Quade's alarm clock came to life. He reached over and shut it off. Snuggling against Kai's back, he closed his eyes once more. He'd been enjoying a delicious dream involving himself and Kai nude on a beach.

He couldn't keep the grin off his face when Kai began to wiggle that cute little ass against Quade's erection. Morning wood had been part of his life since the day he'd hit puberty. He wasn't one of those guys who enjoyed jacking off in the shower. Quade preferred to roll onto his stomach and rub-off against the soft sheets underneath.

Running his hand down Kai's chest, Quade teased the soft skin surrounding his lover's cock. "Mmm," Kai moaned.

"I have to go to work," Quade whispered against Kai's neck. "What do you feel up to doing?"

"Ummm, fucking?" Kai mumbled, the rasp of sleep still in his voice.

Quade smiled. They'd gone at it like rabbits since New Year's Eve, barely bothering to get dressed. "I meant after your morning fuck. When I have to leave."

"I don't know. Has the snow melted?"

A bark of laughter erupted from Quade. "This is Wyoming, Surfer Boy. The snow won't melt until well into spring. The best we can hope for is to keep the roads and sidewalks cleared."

Kai growled deep in his chest. "What do you people do when it's cold like this?"

"Ummm, live? We go on with our normal routine." Quade turned Kai around to face him. "I'll make arrangements to have your rental brought down from the mountain. Maybe you could come by City Hall and let me take you to lunch?"

Kai opened one eye warily. "How far is City Hall?"

"Not far, about three blocks, all flat roads."

"Ice?"

"Nope. You should be good to go." The question reminded Quade he'd need to teach Kai how to drive in the snow and ice. The thought stopped him. Here he was, spinning fantasies again. Kai was a sun lover. No way would the man be content to stay in Cattle Valley. His heart seemed to skip a beat at the realisation. *This is temporary.* Quade knew he had to get that through his hard head.

"I'll meet you. What time?"

"Eleven works for me. It'll give me some time to paw at that sexy body of yours before we venture into the lion's den for lunch."

At Kai's quirked brow, Quade explained. "Our resident chef, Erico, will try his best to steal you away from me."

"Not gonna happen."

"Wait until you meet him. The guy is sex on a stick and knows it. He'll charm the pants right off you given half a chance."

Kai opened his eyes fully and cupped Quade's face in his hands. "In the previous year I've been surrounded by men most would describe as sex on a stick. None of them were the least bit tempting to me. Don't worry."

Even though Kai's reassurance went a long way to put him at ease, Quade knew his lover was right. Kai could have almost anyone he wanted with just a snap of his graceful fingers.

Climbing on top of Quade's chest, Kai straddled him. "Is there a doctor in town?"

Alarmed, Quade searched Kai's face for any signs of distress. "Yeah. Is there something wrong?"

"Yeah. We're almost out of condoms, and I'd rather get tested than buy more." Kai looked out the window. "Unless of course you'd rather not," Kai's voice trailed off.

It was a big step in their budding relationship. Was Kai saying he wanted a strictly monogamous relationship? Did he trust the younger man not to stray when he wasn't around?

"Yeah, sure. There's a clinic downtown. I'll call and make us both appointments," he said, making up his mind to jump headlong into the trust game.

Kai swivelled his hips, grinding his ass against Quade's ever-present morning erection. "Do you have time?" Kai asked.

Quade's gaze drifted to the clock. "I'll make time. Carol will be screeching about something or other anyway. I might as well give the banshee some ammunition that's actually worth the trouble."

Kai laughed. "I can't wait to actually meet that woman. I follow the town newsletters that you put out. It seems the two of you are always on each other's case about something. Why don't you just fire her?"

Quade grinned. "Because I'd be completely lost without the old battleaxe."

Kai leaned over to the table and picked up the bottle of lube. "That's weird, dude."

"Yeah. I've been told that before by most everyone in town."

Quade took the lube from Kai. "Condom?" he asked.

Kai searched the bedside table, flicking the empty wrappers out of the way before coming back with one. "There's only two left. Guess we'll have to get another box after all."

"Damn straight," Quade agreed. "Two won't even last through the evening."

"You're insatiable," Kai cooed.

"Only with you," Quade pulled Kai down for a kiss.

Chapter Five

Bored out of his skull, Kai was trying to find something to watch on TV when the doorbell rang. Hopping up from the couch, he looked through the peephole. Two distorted men stood on the small porch.

After deciding neither of the men looked like serial killers, Kai unlocked and opened the door. "Hi," he greeted.

The much smaller of the two slid past Kai and entered the house. "I'm Nate," he introduced himself. "This is my partner, Rio." Nate pointed to the huge muscular man still standing on the porch.

Kai couldn't believe the guy just walked in without an invitation. "Can I help you?"

Nate grinned. "Nope, but we can help you." He produced a set of keys. "Quade called and asked if we'd drive your rental over."

Relieved that these two men must be friends of Quade's, Kai's mood lifted. "Oh, I'm sorry. Thanks," he said, taking the keys.

The big man on the porch started shifting from foot to foot. "Come in," he hastened to say.

"Thanks," Rio said. "I swear the temperature's dropping by the minute."

After Rio was safely on the large rug in the entry hall, Kai shut the door. "Can I get you something to warm you up? Coffee maybe?" It didn't matter that he knew nothing about the men, but was in need of company.

"If it's not too much trouble, coffee sounds great actually," Nate replied, sliding his feet out of heavy, snow-covered boots.

Kai grinned. *Nothing like just making yourself at home.* "No trouble at all. I'm bored as hell."

Kai looked at the big man still standing on the rug. Nate must have read his thoughts. "Don't worry about Rio. It's a major production for him to get his boots on and off. He'll be fine." Nate stood on his tiptoes and kissed Rio. "I'll bring you a cup."

Rio smiled and nodded, but said nothing. *Interesting.* Kai led the way to the kitchen. "I was just trying to find something on TV, but every channel is too fuzzy to watch," he said over his shoulder, as he prepared the coffee.

"Snow," Nate surmised. "It builds up on the dish and you can't get shit in the way of reception." Nate held up a finger. "Hold on. I'll be right back."

Nate disappeared as Kai finished pouring the water into the automatic coffeemaker. He silently wondered if everyone in Cattle Valley was as odd as the two men in the hall.

"Okay," Nate said, returning to the kitchen. "I sent Rio out to clean off your satellite dish."

Kai was shocked. "Oh, he doesn't have to do that. I can find something else to keep me busy."

Nate held up a hand. "Don't worry about it. He's happier when he has something to do."

Nate slid onto one of the island barstools. "So, exactly what're your intentions towards our mayor?"

Stunned, Kai's jaw dropped. "Uh, I met him on his last trip to Oahu."

"Yeah, yeah, I already know all that. Quade hasn't stopped talking about you since he got back. What I'm curious about is do you see this developing into something permanent?"

Kai wanted to be outraged by the question, but the earnest look on Nate's face stopped his blood pressure from climbing to new heights. Despite not being angry by the question, Kai still didn't know what to say to the older man. In the end, he decided to go with an honest answer. "I care a lot about him. Is that what you're asking?"

Nate seemed to study Kai for several moments. "It'll do. For now," Nate added with a wink.

A loud thumping noise brought Kai's attention to the window. "What was that?"

Nate shrugged and filled an empty cup with coffee. "Rio most likely."

All Kai could imagine was the giant man sprawled out in the snow after falling from the roof. "Should we go check on him?"

At that moment, a giant sheet of ice sailed past the window. Nate chuckled and took a sip of his drink. "He's fine. Rio's an ex-merc," Nate informed him. "It takes a hell of a lot to put him out of commission."

Kai nodded and refilled his own cup from earlier that morning. "I'm supposed to meet Quade at his office at eleven. How early should I plan on leaving?"

"Roads are good. Should only take you about two minutes to get there."

Hearing additional noises coming from the roof, Nate looked towards the ceiling. "Don't ask me what the hell he's doin' up there. I told him to clean off the satellite, but that should've been done ten minutes ago."

Nate stood, finished off his coffee and took the empty cup to the sink. "Thanks for the brew, but we need to get over to The Gym."

"There's a gym in town?" Kai asked, surprised such a small town would have one.

"Yep. Rio and I opened one to keep us out of trouble." Another bang from the roof rattled the windows. "As you can tell, it hasn't done much good," Nate snickered.

The thought of getting some exercise rejuvenated Kai. "If I were to stop by, could I just pay as I go, or would I need to get some kind of membership?"

"Quade's already a member. I'm sure he's got a stack of guest passes around here somewhere. Stop by when you can." Nate walked to the entry hall and stepped into his boots.

"I'll do that."

After Nate left, Kai decided to change his clothes for his lunch date. Digging into his suitcase, he shook his head. Why hadn't he thought to buy appropriate cold-weather clothing? Maybe Quade had something he could borrow?

Instead of assuming, Kai went to the bedside table and picked up the phone. His finger followed the scrolled penmanship of Quade's handwriting on the tablet beside the lamp. Punching in the number written down, Kai waited.

"City Hall," a woman answered.

"Hi. Is Quade busy?"

"Well, that depends on who's calling," the woman declared.

"Oh...um...this is Kai."

"You don't say. I finally get to speak to the man who's responsible for making my life miserable."

"Excuse me?" He knew by the sarcastic tone of the woman's voice, it could be none other than Carol, Quade's secretary. Quade had told him about Carol before, but Kai always thought his lover was exaggerating. Now he wasn't so sure.

"Oh, never mind, I'll put you through," Carol quipped.

"Hey," Quade answered, several moments later.

"Hi. Have I done something to offend Carol?" Kai asked, still reeling from his earlier conversation.

Quade sighed. "Why, what'd she do now?"

"Nothing really," Kai quickly answered. The last thing he wanted was to get the woman fired. "She just mentioned that I was responsible for making her life miserable."

Quade chuckled. "Don't take it personally. She's just had to put up with my grouchy ass since I got back from vacation."

"Do you still want me to meet you there? Because I don't want to cause any more trouble with her." Hell, Carol was scary enough on the phone. The last thing he wanted to do was give the woman a physical target.

"I'll tell her to be good. She's really not as bad as everyone thinks." Quade cleared his throat. "Well she is, but I can usually control her in the right situation."

"Cool," Kai responded. Remembering why he was calling in the first place, Kai looked towards Quade's closet. "Is there a place in town I can buy a few shirts and stuff? I got to looking and all I brought was T's and a couple of dress shirts." Kai chuckled. "I think I'm gonna need something a little warmer."

"Sure. There's a department store downtown. You remember Wyn, from the party?"

"Uh, which one was he?"

"Small, skinny guy sitting next to the guy who resembled Paul Bunyon."

"Oh, yeah, I remember him."

"Well he owns the shop. I'm sure he can get you all fixed up with whatever you need."

"Good." *Come on, just ask him.* "Do you think it would be okay if I borrowed one of your shirts until I can get some?"

"Of course," Quade said. "No need to even ask. Get what you want, but I'll warn you, my stuff is gonna be too big for you."

"Thanks." Kai glanced at the clock. "Let me get off the phone and get changed. I'll be there in less than twenty."

"Looking forward to it. I made us both appointments at the clinic, by the way."

"Oh, cool." Kai hung up the phone and ventured into Quade's huge walk-in closet.

Looking through the large rack of casual shirts, he pulled a red and black checked flannel from its hanger. Shrugging into it, he quickly determined Quade had been right. His much smaller frame was practically swallowed by the over-sized garment. Making do, Kai rolled the sleeves up a couple of times and left it unbuttoned. With his white T-shirt underneath, it looked more like a jacket, but it would have to do.

After running a brush through his hair, Kai picked up the keys and pulled on his borrowed coat and boots. Looking at himself in the hall mirror, he shook his head. It was a damn good thing he was in love, because he doubted he'd go through this for anyone other than Quade.

Bracing himself against the cold, Kai opened the door. He was locking up when he realised he'd forgotten to look for gloves. "Shit." Kai thought about going back inside, but nixed the idea. Hopefully they wouldn't be outside much. He could just stick his hands in his coat pockets.

By the time he got to his rented SUV and fastened his seatbelt, he was starting to rethink his decision. His hands were beet red and stiff. Cupping them in front of his face, Kai blew warm air into them like he'd seen people do on television. He was surprised how much it helped.

Pulling out of the driveway, Kai drove the three blocks to City Hall. Despite what Nate had told him, Kai didn't find the roads to be clear at all. The dry crunch of packed snow under the tires proved it. He decided to take his time and drive at a speed he was comfortable with. It wasn't until a car horn sounded behind him that he realised he'd only been travelling at fifteen miles per hour.

After what felt like a long trip, he pulled into the parking lot. He decided he might be better off walking home. Maybe he'd just turn in the rental. No sense in paying for something he was too scared to use.

Walking up the steps, he opened the front double doors. A plaque on the wall pointed him to the mayor's office. Bracing himself, he stepped into the reception area and came face to face with the dragon lady.

"You must be Kai," Carol said, looking over the top of her glasses at him.

"Yes, Ma'am," Kai replied, blowing on his hands again. The first order of business was to get a damn pair of gloves.

Carol came out from behind her desk and looked Kai up and down. "You're even cuter than your picture," she commented.

"Uh, thank you?" He didn't know what else to say. *What picture?*

"In here, Kai," Quade called through the open doorway.

Kai looked towards the voice and saw Quade with his hand over the phone's mouthpiece. With a brief nod to Carol, Kai tried to make his escape.

"Don't hurt him," Carol warned, walking back to her desk.

Kai stepped into the office, and Quade motioned for him to shut the door. Glad to put a barrier between himself and Carol, Kai immediately did as asked. He stayed where he was and looked down at his snow covered boots.

"Okay," Quade said into the phone. "Get back to me when you find out." Quade hung up the phone and smiled. "Come here."

Kai pointed down. "I'm all snowy."

"Don't worry about it." Quade stood and met Kai halfway. "How was your morning?" Quade asked, before giving Kai a kiss.

"Good. I met your friends Nate and Rio."

Quade chuckled. "Quite a pair, aren't they?"

"They seemed nice. Though I didn't get much of a chance to talk to Rio. I mentioned that I couldn't get reception on the TV, and Nate sent the poor guy up on the roof to knock the snow off the satellite."

"Typical," Quade remarked.

Quade reached down to hold Kai's hands and stopped. "What the hell?" He lifted Kai's frozen hands and placed gentle kisses on each one. "You couldn't find any gloves?"

Kai shrugged. "I forgot about gloves until I was outside with the house already locked up. I figured I'd just stick them in my pockets."

Quade's brow quirked up. "And do you still think that was a wise decision?"

"Let's just say gloves are my first priority on the shopping list."

Releasing him, Quade walked over to his desk and looked in a small book. "I don't have any meetings scheduled this afternoon. I think I'll take an extra long lunch. We can stop at Wyn's on the way to the restaurant. Your bits are too precious to get frostbite."

Kai wasn't exactly sure what frostbite was exactly, but it didn't sound like anything he wanted to happen to his bits. "Definitely clothes first, then."

Chapter Six

"So, do you feel like walking to the Canoe, or would you rather I drive?" Quade asked, leading Kai down the steps of City Hall.

Kai seemed to weigh the pros and cons of both. "I think we should drive. At least until I can get some gloves."

"Shit, babe, I'm sorry." Quade took off his gloves and handed them to Kai.

"I'm not gonna take those," Kai declared, shaking his head.

Quade pressed them into Kai's hands and kissed him. "Yes you are. I'm used to the cold. You're not."

With a roll of his eyes, Kai eventually slipped the gloves on. "Sorry," Kai mumbled.

"No need." Quade kissed his lover again. "I'd give you the shirt off my back if you needed it."

Kai chuckled and pulled at the collar under his coat. "You already have."

"So? Walking?" Quade noticed Kai's entire body shaking from the unaccustomed temperatures. "No. I think we'll drive."

Kai nodded and they walked hand in glove towards the Escalade. "I know I said we'd go to the Canoe, but I just got an idea. Why don't we go to Deb's Diner for lunch, and I'll take you to the fancier digs for dinner?"

"Sounds fine to me," Kai answered, getting into the SUV.

Quade managed to find a parking spot in front of the diner. "Rock Star parking," he chuckled.

Deb acknowledged Quade as soon as they stepped foot in the door. "Back booth's open," she yelled over the crowd.

With a wave, he pulled Kai along behind him to the booth. "It gets kinda crazy in here around lunchtime," he mentioned, as Kai sat across from him.

Kai smiled and opened a menu that was already sitting on the table. "What's good?"

"Anything. Everything," Quade added. "You can never go wrong with the special of the day. Monday is meatloaf day. You can either have it cold on a sandwich or hot with potatoes and gravy."

Kai's nose scrunched up. "Do they have any fish?"

Quade should've known Kai wouldn't enjoy anything heavy. The man was an athlete. "I wouldn't suggest the fish here, but the Canoe has quite a few fantastic seafood items on their menu."

Kai nodded, still pouring over the menu. "I think I'll just stick with soup and salad." Kai reached down and rubbed his stomach. "Save the big meal for later."

A pain shot through Quade's chest. He didn't know why it bothered him so much that Kai didn't appear to care for the food choices at Deb's, but it did. Maybe he wanted the younger man to fall in love with Cattle Valley as he had on his first visit. The cold weather was already a different strike against the community, and now it seemed the food was another.

"Is something wrong?" Kai asked.

"No," Quade answered.

"Well, you look like someone snaked your wave. Would you rather I try the special?"

Quade reached across the table and entwined his fingers with Kai's. "Not at all. You get what'll make you happy."

"It's just a salad, dude. Can't say the lettuce or the meatloaf will make me happy." Kai lifted and kissed Quade's hand. "You make me happy. The rest is just filler."

His lightening mood was interrupted by Deb, order pad in hand. "Hi, Sugar, what can I get the two of you?" the middle-aged woman asked.

"I'll take the special, sandwich-style, with a Dr. Pepper and side of fries." After he ordered he thought better of it. "Change the fries to a side salad."

Deb's eyebrow shot to her hairline as she amended his order and turned to Kai. "What can I get ya, Cutey?"

As Kai ordered his lunch with the dressing on the side, Quade made a new resolve, if he was going to keep up with the younger man for the next thirty or forty years, he needed to start eating healthier. He wasn't out of shape by any stretch of the imagination, but Quade knew he could do better. The closer he crept to forty, the more he realised exercising a couple of times a week wasn't enough.

After Deb hurried off with their order, Kai slid out of the booth and stood next to the table looking down at Quade. "Would you mind if I sat beside you?"

Surprised, Quade shook his head and scooted over. "Not at all."

How many times had he watched couples enjoying each other's company in this very diner? With Kai's warmth pressed against his side, Quade felt truly at peace for the first time in a long time. He lifted his arm and wrapped it around Kai's shoulder, giving the man a sideways hug. "This is nice."

"Yeah," Kai agreed. Kai's eyes roamed around the room. "People seem pretty nice here."

"They are," Quade stated. He shifted in his seat when Kai's hand landed on his thigh.

"What're you thinking so hard about?" Kai asked.

Quade shrugged. "Stuff. It's hard to believe you're actually here. Do you know how many lunches I've spent at this very booth, wishing I had you beside me?"

Kai leaned over and placed a soft kiss to Quade's neck, just below his ear. "Do you know how many times I sat on the beach, looking out at the sunset, wishing I had you there to enjoy it with me?"

"I do love a nice sunset." Quade felt relieved that he wasn't the only one pining during their months apart.

"I know." Kai snuggled even closer to whisper in Quade's ear. "I'm sorry I'm not fitting in like I wanted."

Quade's eyes drifted shut. He evidently wasn't doing such a bang up job of hiding his disappointment. "It's not your fault. You were raised in a completely different environment. It doesn't help that you came to visit at possibly the worst time of the year. Who knows, you might really enjoy the other three seasons?"

Kai smiled. "Yeah. I'll definitely have to make a trip back in the summer. The rodeo you've talked about sounds awesome."

There it was, that stab of pain again. Kai wasn't planning on staying. *Hell, I already knew that.* So why did it hurt so much to actually hear Kai confirm his fears?

Deb set their food down in front of them, and Quade tried to push the oncoming depression away. There would be plenty of time to mourn Kai when he was gone. Best to enjoy what little time he'd been given.

* * * *

Holding the cotton ball to the crook of his arm, Kai waited for Quade. He grinned as Quade's face scrunched up with the needle insertion. He hadn't known how much his lover hated all things hospital until they'd arrived at the clinic. The fact that Quade was willing to undergo a blood test spoke volumes to Kai. *He really does love me.*

He hated the haunted look in his man's eyes over lunch. As much as Kai loved surfing, he was starting to believe his feelings for Quade were even stronger. Was he actually thinking about giving up his career?

"All done," the technician announced.

"Whew!" Quade exclaimed. "I thought I might pass out there for a minute."

Chuckling, Kai put on his coat and waited by the door. "Where to now?" he asked, as they left the clinic.

"Wyn's is right down the street. Feel up to walking?"

"Sure," Kai agreed.

Before they reached the store, Quade's cell phone rang. He looked at Kai apologetically. "Sorry."

"No problem."

Quade answered his phone as they walked. "What?" Quade yelled, sticking his finger in his ear to block out the traffic noise. "Shit! Okay, I'll drive over."

Closing his phone, Quade pointed towards their destination. "Will you be okay by yourself for a while? We've had a water-line break and the city engineer seems to think the whole damn pipe needs replacing."

"I'll be fine," Kai assured Quade, giving him a quick kiss.

"Stop by my office after you're done shopping."

"Sounds good," Kai said. "Oh wait, take these." Kai removed the borrowed gloves and held them out.

Accepting them, Quade gave him one more kiss before pulling away. Kai watched his lover jog down and across the street to his Escalade. Shaking his head, Kai opened the door to Wyn's Department Store.

* * * *

As he stood on the sidewalk an hour later, Kai couldn't believe the difference proper winter clothing made. Suddenly the day didn't seem nearly as cold as it had before. Looking up and down Main Street, he decided to do a little window shopping before heading back to Quade's office. He promised the clerk at the store he'd be back to pick up his bags before they closed, so until then, he was free to do as he pleased.

A store across the street caught his eye. *Flowers.* He missed seeing them. Deciding to get a bouquet of them for Quade as a surprise, he checked traffic before jogging over. A little brass bell over the door signalled his arrival upon stepping foot into the shop.

Kai was greeted by a kind face with sad brown eyes. "Hi," Kai greeted.

"Hello," the man said in return. "Is there something I can help you with?"

Kai's eyes roamed the store. Besides flowers, there were plants, vases and other small decorating items on display. "I'm visiting a friend of mine and thought I'd surprise him with flowers."

The brown-eyed man stepped from behind the counter. "You must be Kai. I'm Tyler," the man informed him, holding out his hand.

Kai shook it, puzzled. "Word must travel fast. I've only been in town for a couple of days."

Tyler smiled. "I could chalk it up to gossip, but the truth is, I had a meeting with Quade earlier and he mentioned you were here." Tyler motioned towards the refrigerated display case. "Is there something in particular you're looking for?"

"Tropical? I thought it would help Quade ready himself for his vacation." Kai perused the flowers on display. There didn't seem to be many things with a tropical feel. "Of course I could always go with something more traditional."

Tyler crossed his arms and tapped his finger to his chin, evidently thinking. "How about both? Like the combination of you and Quade."

Kai had no idea how daisies and tropical flowers would mix, but he decided to trust the expert. "If you think it'll look good, sure."

He watched as Tyler began taking buckets of flowers out of the cooler and setting them on his work station. "You might want to take your coat off if you're going to wait," Tyler said. "Or I can always deliver them for you?"

Kai inhaled the sweet perfume of air. "Do you mind if I watch, but still have you deliver them? I'm on foot, and I'm not sure how long they'd survive out in the cold."

Tyler grinned, selecting a vase from off the shelf. "Probably a lot longer than you would," he teased. "But yeah, I'd be happy to have the company."

"Not much business this time of year?" Kai inquired.

Tyler shook his head. "Practically dead. If it weren't for Hearn and his weekly standing order, I'd probably just shut down for the month."

"Wow. Someone buys his partner a bouquet every week? That's true love," Kai remarked.

Before he'd even finished his sentence, Kai noticed Tyler's eyes tearing up. "I'm sorry. Did I say something wrong?"

Tyler stared off into space for several moments before blinking the tears away. "No. Sorry." Tyler cleared his throat as he began to build the bouquet. "Hearn puts flowers on his deceased partner's grave every week."

"Oh. Oh, crap. I'm sorry. I didn't mean to sound insensitive," Kai apologised, wanting to kick himself.

"You weren't," Tyler assured him.

With the air in the small room suddenly a whole lot thicker, Kai dug out his wallet. "I just remembered that I'm supposed to meet Quade back at his office. Can I go ahead and pay for those before getting out of your hair?"

"Sure," Tyler replied, trying to smile. "Would you like to fill out a card?" Tyler pointed to the small rack.

After writing a short note to Quade, Kai paid for his purchase. "It was nice to meet you."

"You too," Tyler said.

Kai's hand was on the door handle when movement out the window caught his eyes. There, standing not ten feet away, was Nate kissing a man who most definitely wasn't Rio. *Dammit.* He'd really liked Nate, too.

"Is everything okay?" Tyler asked from the counter.

Kai didn't want to call any more attention to the cheating couple on the sidewalk. "Yes. I was just psyching myself up for the cold."

Tyler chuckled. "Good luck with that."

As he spoke to Tyler, Kai watched as the two men on the sidewalk separated and went in opposite directions. With a sigh of relief, Kai opened the door and headed to Quade. The long-haired man Nate had been kissing walked about a half of a block in front of him. Kai studied the man as he made his way to City Hall.

Whoever the hell Nate was cheating with seemed to be a member of the Sheriff's Department, at least according to the back of the guy's coat. Kai watched him warily until he turned and entered the police station.

He couldn't help but to feel sick to his stomach. There was just something about cheating men that he despised. Never had he considered cheating on a guy. It didn't matter if the fling lasted a weekend or a month.

Climbing the steps to Quade's office, he wondered if he should mention it to his lover? He knew Nate and Rio were Quade's friends. The last thing he wanted was to destroy a relationship, but on the other hand, Rio seemed like such a gentle giant, and Kai hated to see the big man duped.

Maybe he'd wait and discuss it with Quade over dinner. It would at least give him more time to work up the courage. Hopefully, Quade wouldn't take the news of his friend's infidelity too badly.

Another thought struck him. *What if Quade knows and isn't doing anything about it?* Kai shook his head. No. If Quade knew he'd definitely do something about it. If he didn't, he wasn't the man Kai thought he was.

Chapter Seven

"Look at you, Mr. Lumberjack!" Quade exclaimed, as Kai entered his office.

Kai took off his coat and hung it on the rack. "You approve?" he asked, striking various modelling poses. He made sure to give Quade several good views of his ass.

"I likey." Quade pushed his chair away from his desk. "I assume Carol made you take off your boots at the outer door?"

Kai rolled his eyes and pointed towards his socks. Chuckling, Quade held out his arms. "Shut the door and come over here."

Without turning around, Kai shut the door. "Should I lock it?"

"Naw. Carol knows she'd burn her retinas if she were to barge in." He winked. "Isn't that right, Carol?!" he yelled.

"Shut up!" Carol screamed in reply.

Kai shook his head. "You two have got the weirdest relationship on the planet."

"Yeah, but we look out for each other." Quade spread his thighs and cupped his cock. "My lap is lonely."

"You don't say." Kai sauntered over and curled up on Quade's lap. "How'd the water thingy turn out?"

Quade ran his hands under Kai's ass and squeezed. "Do you really care?" he asked, lips touching Kai's.

He knew he could be supportive and tell Quade that everything he did concerned him, but the truth was he couldn't care less at the moment. What he did care about was the bulge growing behind his lover's fly. Instead of answering the question, Kai closed the distance and kissed those sweet lips in front of him.

Quade opened to Kai's exploring tongue on contact, and Kai took full advantage, sweeping the interior like a man dying of thirst. Without thought, Kai began to unbutton Quade's shirt, needing the warm feel of his lover's skin.

Quade's hands joined Kai's in hastening the task. Kai moaned into the kiss as he ran his hands over Quade's muscled torso. "God you feel good," he said, pulling out of the kiss. He scooted off Quade's lap and licked his way down his lover's neck to suckle first one nipple before moving on to the other.

Kai felt the rumble in Quade's chest as the man groaned. "You make me feel like a king," Quade panted, as Kai's hands began unfastening his pants.

Quade lifted his hips, as Kai's hand gripped the stiff erection hidden inside. "You're my Kahuna," Kai whispered, kissing his way down to Quade's lap. Before he could wrap his lips around the large bulbous head, a stream of pre-cum ran down Kai's fist. "Mmm," he moaned, licking the salty essence from his fingers.

Kai's eyes remained transfixed on another large drop of pre-cum poised to fall. Before it had a chance to cascade down the heavily veined shaft, Kai sucked the crown into his mouth. Relaxing his throat, Kai impaled his mouth on Quade's cock. It took two attempts, but Kai was able to swallow Quade's entire length.

"Aahh, fuck!" Quade howled, grabbing the sides of Kai's head.

Giving up control, Kai groaned as his man began fucking his throat in earnest, the sounds of their mutual pleasure reverberating through the office. Kai reached down and unzipped his jeans, fisting himself.

"Love you," Quade groaned, hips snapping, grip on Kai's hair tightening.

Bracing himself for his prize, Kai was rewarded with a flood of cum. The first shot went straight down his throat without giving Kai the chance to taste it. Backing off Quade's length, the next volley landed on his tongue. The flavour exploded in Kai's mouth, triggering his own release.

He started to pull off his lover's cock too soon and ended up shot in the face. Kai grinned and looked up at Quade, cum dripping down his lips and chin. "Got me," he chuckled.

With heavy-lidded eyes, Quade pulled Kai back up to sit in his lap. With his hands still buried in Kai's hair, Quade licked his own cum from Kai's face. "Fuck that's hot," Kai whispered.

Quade followed the tongue bath with a deep kiss. "That was better than any fantasy I've ever woven in this office."

"It could be better. I could let you bend me over your desk and fuck my brains out," Kai informed.

"I can hear you," Carol called out in a loud, sing-songy voice.

Kai looked at Quade. "Oops."

Quade started to laugh, before long, Kai joined in. A loud banging on the wall had them laughing even harder until tears sprung to Kai's eyes. He knew he should be embarrassed, but with all the crap Carol seemed to enjoy dishing out, she deserved a big plateful in return.

Drying his eyes, Kai stood. "I need to go. I promised I'd be back to pick up the clothes I bought." Besides, he didn't want to be there when Tyler delivered Quade's flowers. He'd never sent a lover flowers and didn't know what Quade's reaction would be.

Quade's eyes were riveted on Kai's cock as he tucked it away and zipped up. "Will you come back to your place and pick me up, or are you gonna make me brave the streets again?"

"Oh, so you were the one who was blocking traffic earlier?"

"One car. It was one car," Kai shot back defensively. "What'd the guy do? Call you?"

Quade started to laugh all over again. "I was totally kidding. You just busted yourself, babe."

Exasperated, Kai swatted Quade on the arm. "Kiss me quick. I'm leaving."

Quade pulled Kai down for a kiss, but it was anything but quick. It was Kai's turn to have the interior of his mouth explored. Kai wondered if Quade was searching for remnants of his own seed.

"Wow." Kai stood and did an all-over body shake, trying to dispel the sudden surge of lust. "So? Pick me up? I'll make it worth your while," he cooed.

"I'll be home at five," Quade answered, zipping his pants. "Be naked. We can eat a late dinner."

Kai shook his head. "No way. Dinner first. Otherwise we won't ever leave the house."

Quade rubbed his chin. "Okay, deal. But you'll owe me," Quade added.

"More than you'll ever know," Kai said, and opened the door to the outer office.

He tried his best to ignore the growl coming from the desk across from him as he slid into his boots. Bundled against the weather, he turned and gave the secretary a playful wink. "He should be in a good mood for the rest of the day. If you wanted some time off or a raise, now's the time to ask."

* * * *

"Damn. I'm glad I made reservations," Quade said, finding a spot on the side of the restaurant to park.

"Is it usually this busy?" Kai asked, looking at all the cars. Hell, he didn't even know there were this many people in Cattle Valley.

"Fridays and Saturdays, yeah, but not normally during the week. Everyone must be sick of being stuck indoors."

Kai got out and walked beside Quade around the side to the front of the Canoe. A scene in the window caught his eyes and his steps faltered. There, right behind the plate glass, was Nate and that guy he was kissing earlier. Kai couldn't believe Nate would be as bold as that with an affair.

"Cute, aren't they?" Quade asked, taking notice of the pair Kai was staring at.

"Cute?" He couldn't believe what he was hearing. "You think that's cute?"

Quade flushed. "Okay, hot."

Even more stunned, Kai spun away from the cheating view and walked up the steps to the restaurant. Did he know the man behind him at all? How in the world could Quade think infidelity was hot?

"Hey." He heard a deep familiar voice come up behind him.

Kai glanced over his shoulder to find Rio climbing the steps. Shit. "Hey," he said, turning to block the door. He didn't know how he was going to manage it, but he had to get Rio away from the restaurant. The last thing the big guy deserved was to come face to face with the nightmare inside.

"I think they're all booked. Why don't you try the diner, or the lodge?" he offered, trying to think on his feet.

Rio gave him a confused expression. "That's okay. I've got reservations. But thanks."

Kai looked around Rio to Quade and begged him for help using his eyes instead of his mouth. When his lover just looked at him like he was crazy, and Rio tried to move past him, Kai's hand shot out and braced itself on Rio's chest. "Seriously, you don't want to go in there."

Rio glanced down at Kai's hand and shot him an unfriendly look. "Is there a problem?" Rio asked.

Quade tried to step between the two men. "Kai? What's going on? Let the man go inside."

Could this get any worse? "Do you really want him to go in and see Nate and that other guy?" he whispered in Quade's ear.

"Yeah," Quade said innocently. "That's why he's here."

Quade removed Kai's hand from Rio's chest. "Sorry about that," he said to Rio.

At a complete loss, Kai stepped back and threw up his hands as Rio squeezed by him. In utter disgust, Kai started back down the steps towards the SUV.

"Wait!" Quade called after him. "Where the hell are you going?"

Quade caught up with Kai at the bottom of the stairs. "I can't go in there," he declared, crossing his arms.

"Why?"

"I can't stand by and watch what'll happen when Rio sees Nate and the other guy."

Quade's attention went to the window behind Kai. "Why do you have such a problem with it? Of all people, I'd think you would be open about something like that."

"What's that supposed to mean?" Kai yelled, giving Quade's chest a push.

Quade's face turned red. Kai could tell the push had pissed the man off, but at that point, he couldn't have cared less. Reaching out, Quade took Kai by the shoulders and spun him to face the window. "Now you tell me, what the hell is wrong with that? Those men love each other!"

Kai's eyes almost crossed at the scene in front of him. Rio, Nate and the other guy were all sitting at the table sharing kisses and holding hands. "What the fuck," he mumbled. "Rio's not pissed to find his partner on a date with another man?"

A bark of laughter erupted over his shoulder. Kai turned and looked up at Quade. "What's so funny?"

"I can't believe I didn't catch on earlier. Come with me," Quade ordered. He led Kai by the hand back up the steps and inside the restaurant. "Hold that thought," he said to the host at the door.

Quade pulled Kai to stand by the table they had just been outside ogling. "Kai, I'd like you to meet Sheriff Ryan Blackfeather, Nate and Rio's *partner*."

"Partner?" Kai squeaked. "Aww, damn. I'm sorry." God he felt like such an ass.

He felt even worse when Ryan stood and stuck out his hand. "Great to finally meet you, Kai. I've heard a lot of good things about you."

Kai shook the tattooed man's hand, but couldn't quite meet his gaze. He glanced over at Rio. "I'm sorry for earlier. I didn't know the three of you were together. I…didn't want you to get hurt."

"Oh my God he's so cute," Nate declared, standing to wrap his arms around Kai. A deep throat cleared from Rio's direction, and Nate released him. "Be nice. He was worried about you," he scolded the big man.

Kai felt two inches tall. He'd humiliated not only himself, but probably Quade as well. He reached out and took his lover's hand. "Sorry if I embarrassed you."

Quade leaned in and kissed him. "You didn't. I agree with Nate. You are cute."

* * * *

Quade looked across the table at the love of his life. Despite what Kai had thought earlier, Quade was proud of his lover. It was comforting to know the younger man felt so strongly about infidelity. It spoke volumes for a future relationship, even if it had to be a long-distance one.

He watched as Kai's perfect pink tongue slid out to lick his lips. "The food was fantastic," Kai commented.

"Yeah," he agreed. "Your scallops were okay?"

"More than okay. Thanks for bringing me."

Quade stretched his hand across the table and was delighted when Kai held it. "I love you," Quade declared.

Kai smiled, the candlelight dancing in his lover's eyes. "I love you too."

Quade stood enough to lean over the table and placed a soft kiss on Kai's lips. "Ready?"

Before Kai could answer, his cell phone began playing Wipe Out. The younger man looked surprised when he glanced at the display. "Do you mind if I take this? It's my dad."

"Not at all. I'll take care of the cheque." Quade watched as Kai rose and put the phone to his ear as he walked towards the restrooms.

He signalled to the server for their cheque. As he waited, he wondered why Kai's dad would be calling. From the previous weekend, Quade knew that Kai called daily to check in with his folks. A thought struck him. *Shit.* He hoped nothing was wrong with Kai's mother, brother or sister.

After paying the bill, he finished off his bourbon. It was another fifteen minutes before Kai returned to the table. His lover had a lost look on his face.

"What happened?" Quade asked, standing to pull Kai into his arms.

"Can we talk about it when we get back to your place?" Kai mumbled.

Quade's chest felt so tight he could barely breathe by the time they climbed into the Escalade. He started the SUV and turned to Kai. "Tell me," he begged.

Kai looked at Quade with tears in his eyes. "I think I need to go home."

"Why, what happened? Is someone sick?" Quade asked feeling frantic.

"No. My dad gave me a message. Van Duggins called my parents' house looking for me. Dad took his number and promised I'd call right back, so I did."

"And? Who is this Van guy?"

"The greatest surfer Hawaii ever produced. He's a transplant, like me. Grew up on the island and learned to surf like a native by the age of ten."

Quade reached over and lifted Kai to sit in his lap. "What did this guy want?"

"To teach me. He's only done it a time or two in the past. Those that he's taken an interest in have gone on to win every tournament they've entered. It's been over ten years since he's trained someone, but for some reason, he chose me." Kai's tearful gaze met Quade's. "It's the chance of a lifetime, but it also means leaving you."

"When exactly? I mean, you don't have to leave now, do you?"

Kai's chin dropped to his chest. "Couple days, probably Friday. The season starts the third week in February with an Australian tournament. That only gives me a little over a month to soak up everything I can from Van."

Friday? Quade hugged Kai tightly to his chest. He didn't even want to think about his lover leaving him, but what kind of man would he be if he stood in the way of Kai's greatness. "Go," he finally said, feeling tears escape his eyes.

Chapter Eight

Friday came too damn soon for Quade. He tapped his fingers on the steering wheel as he waited for Kai to return his SUV at the rental agency. He tried like hell to memorise every feature of the younger man as he stared at him through the glass. *I'll see him again within a month.*

After the night Kai had told him about Van, Quade had gone online to look the guy up. That's when his real worries had started. Though older than Quade by almost eleven years, Van Duggins still looked amazing. The fact that the man was an idol to Kai made it even worse. What if the teacher tried to teach more than surfing techniques to his student? Would Kai be able to resist?

"Sorry that took so long," Kai apologised, climbing into the passenger seat.

"Don't worry. Your flight doesn't leave for another two hours," Quade said with a heavy heart.

Kai's hand landed on his thigh. "If you don't want me to go…"

Quade threaded his fingers through Kai's and squeezed. He wanted so much to get on his knees and beg his lover to stay. He'd thought all week about doing that very thing, but he kept coming back to the same conclusion.

If Kai didn't take advantage of this opportunity, the younger man would come to resent Quade for it. The last thing Quade wanted was to see the 'what ifs' in Kai's eyes for the rest of their lives. "No. You need to go. I'll join you soon."

Quade lifted Kai's hand and kissed it. "Just remember how much I love you." *And please don't fall in love with Van*, he added silently.

Putting the Escalade into gear, Quade pulled out of the parking lot. "I thought we might have time for a drink before you have to go through security."

"Okay," Kai responded, gazing out the side window. "I can't believe how much snow falls here," Kai murmured.

"We don't always get this much. The blizzard that blew through was the first of its kind in over twenty years," he defended.

Kai simply shrugged his shoulders without turning to face Quade. The hand on the steering wheel gripped the leather covered plastic until his knuckles were white. Why did he feel the need to make excuses for his home?

Within minutes, Quade pulled into the airport and found a parking spot. He felt completely numb. A small part of him wished Kai had never come to Cattle Valley in the first place. Before New Year's Eve,

Quade had been miserable, but it was nothing to the way he felt at that moment.

"This is it," he choked.

"Yeah," Kai agreed, making no move to get out.

"Will you call me when you get home?" Quade asked.

"Probably not right away. It'll be the middle of the night here," Kai answered, finally turning to face Quade.

Quade noticed the moisture pooling in his lover's brown eyes. "I don't care what time it is. I won't rest until I know you're safely on the ground."

Quade's chest hitched as his own tears started to form. He gasped for a breath as he pulled Kai across the console. "I love you so much," he cried, burying his face in Kai's neck to hide his tears. There was so much he wanted to say, but the words remained frozen in his throat.

Kai hugged him back. "I love you too." Kai kissed the side of Quade's head.

* * * *

"I'm worried about you," Carol divulged, sitting in the chair in front of Quade's desk.

Quade looked up from the stack of papers. "I'm okay."

"No, you're not," Carol returned. "You're not eating. You're not sleeping." She reached across the desk and touched Quade's hand. "It looks like you've aged ten years in the past two weeks."

"Gee, thanks," he drawled. "Kai should be super excited to see me next week."

Carol patted his hand several times. "Why don't you see if you can change your flight? I can cover for you an extra week."

Quade looked down at the papers. "Thanks, but these budget reports have to be finished before I can leave. It'll take me at least a week to get them done."

"Not if I help," Carol offered.

Shocked, Quade stared at his secretary. "Am I dying? Or hearing things?" he tried to joke.

"Neither. I'm just worried." Carol seemed to realise what she'd divulged. Before his eyes, she squared her shoulders and stood. "If you don't want my help, fine. Do it yourself."

She started to walk off, but Quade stopped her. "Yeah, I do. It would help a lot."

Carol spun back to face him. "Very well. Get your shit together, and let me know what I need to do. I'll be at my desk." With that, Carol turned and left the office.

Quade heard his friend's loud sigh as she took her seat. He couldn't stop the grin that replaced his earlier frown. He began sifting through the pages of numbers, trying to figure out how best to utilise the offered help.

As long as the days had been, the nights had been absolute torture since Kai's departure. He'd talked to his lover every evening, but Quade still wasn't sure if it helped or hurt the longing he felt for the younger man.

Kai would begin the calls by giving Quade a rundown of everything he'd learned that day. He'd go on and on about Van and how the legendary surfer was fine-tuning his skills. Quade wanted to hear about

Kai's day, but every time his lover mentioned Van, Quade saw red.

He trusted Kai, he really did. Quade knew the younger man would never intentionally cheat on him, but things happened, unexpected situations popped up. *Stop it!* Quade admonished himself, scrubbing his hands over his face.

Shaking off the unwanted thoughts, Quade went back to his budget sheets. He'd work his ass off for the next couple of days and fly out, that was the best he could do.

* * * *

With his board on the beach, Kai went through the position again.

"NO!" Van screamed. "Where the hell is your head? I've shown you the correct stance three times."

Kai stepped off his board and turned to his mentor. "Sorry. I guess my head's not in it."

"Well shake off whatever's bothering you and get to work. You've only got two and a half weeks to get this right."

Kai nodded and resumed his training. He'd been out of his head with worry since the previous evening. Quade was always there for their nightly phone calls. Where had his lover been that he hadn't answered? Kai had even tried Quade's cell with no luck. He'd left several messages on both phones, but Quade still hadn't called.

Kai had heard the sadness in the older man's voice since he'd left Cattle Valley. Maybe Quade decided a long-distance relationship wasn't worth the pain. What if he'd moved on?

He was brought out of his worries when he was pushed off the board and into the sand. "That was a wave," Van ground out. "You'll never last against the Australian current if you can't plant your body properly."

Kai stayed where he was for a few moments. He was bruised, sore and damned irritated at the way Van coached. He knew Van was the best for a reason. Kai had begun to wonder if he wanted to win enough to continue the torture.

"Is there a problem?" a familiar voice asked.

Kai scrambled out of the sand to face Quade. "Oh my God. What're you doing here?" he asked, launching himself into his lover's strong arms.

Quade gave Kai a short but deep kiss. Pulling back, he gazed into Kai's eyes. "Are you okay?"

"I am now," Kai grinned. He could feel the tension in Quade's shoulders as his lover continued to stare at Van. "Just a lesson. No big deal," he excused Van's behaviour.

"Are you the reason I've been wasting my time all day?" Van asked, crossing his arms.

Quade glanced back at Kai. "Is something else bothering you?"

Kai bit his bottom lip and shrugged. "You weren't home when I tried to call."

Smiling, Quade kissed Kai again. "I was trying to get to the love of my life. I called as soon as I landed, but your phone is evidently off, so I took a chance you'd be here."

"You did."

"Aww, this is touching, but can we get back to work?" Van asked, sneering at Kai and Quade.

Kai wanted to scream no, but he knew he couldn't. He pulled Quade's head down so he could whisper in his ear. "Do you mind if I finish up here? It shouldn't take more than an hour or so."

"Not at all. I'd love to watch you." Quade gave Kai another kiss before releasing him.

Turning back to his coach, Kai nodded. "Okay. I'm ready."

* * * *

With his shirt off and his jeans rolled up, Quade reclined in the warm sand and watched Van put Kai through his drills. He hadn't lied when he'd told Kai he didn't mind watching, but not for the reason his lover thought.

Quade not only wanted to observe the way student and teacher interacted, but he wanted to be there in case Van decided to shove Kai again. He'd almost come completely unglued when he'd seen Kai hit the sand earlier. The surf-god was damn lucky he still had all those pearly white teeth in his head.

The play of Kai's muscles as he paddled out into the ocean, had Quade's cock taking notice. He rolled to his stomach, feeling the sand abrade his tender chest. With his chin resting on his hands, he watched Kai disappear and then reappear as he ducked himself and his board under the oncoming waves.

A nice-sized crowd had begun to gather on the beach to watch. At least Kai wore board shorts instead of those tiny flossed things he was fond of. Quade's gaze moved to Van. Standing on the beach with his bronzed hands on his hips, Van Duggins was quite breathtaking. He wondered if the man had made a play for Kai? There appeared to be tension between Van and Kai, but was it sexual?

The crowd started making noise, and Quade's attention went back to Kai. His lover was up and riding one hell of a wave. One thing was suddenly clear. Van was indeed helping Kai. The younger man's form and finesse were better than ever.

Once the wave died, Kai sat and straddled his board. Van gave him a thumbs up. After gaining his coach's approval, Kai appeared to look at Quade. Sitting up, Quade raised his hands over his head and applauded along with the crowd. He could see Kai's brilliant smile from where he sat.

"He's good," Van said, walking over to where Quade sat.

"Yeah. I know," Quade agreed.

Van stood above Quade looking down. "You being here gonna pose a problem?"

"No."

Van's eyes continued to track Kai. "He can have everything he's ever wanted if he commits himself. Kai doesn't have time for a relationship. It'll only drag him down."

"I won't get in his way. I know how much he wants to be the best. Right now I think that support means something to him."

"Maybe," Van mused. "But what happens when he's so busy thinking about you that his concentration slips and he eats the reef? Will he still think of you the same, knowing his career is over because of you?"

Quade tilted his head and studied the older man. "Are we talking about Kai, or you?"

Van eventually looked down at Quade. "We're talking about professional surfers. We're all alike in many ways."

Without another word, Van strode down the beach. "Tell Kai we're done for the day," Van yelled over his shoulder.

Quade watched Van until the older man rounded a stand of volcanic rock. He started to chuckle when water rained down on his heated back. Turning over, he smiled at Kai, shaking the salt water from his hair. "Van says you're done for the day," Quade informed.

"It's about time," Kai quipped. "Do you know how embarrassing it is trying to work out with a boner? All I kept thinking about was getting you back to my place."

Van's words came back to smack Quade in the face. "The ocean's dangerous. You should keep your mind on what you're doing."

"Sure, in theory. But it's not easy when all you're thinking about is having your lover's cock buried inside you." Kai held out his hand. "Come on. I've waited long enough."

As Quade rose from the sand, he hoped to hell he was doing the right thing. Even the thought of walking away from Kai tore at his heart. But if Van's words proved true, Quade knew he would. Risking Kai's career and safety weren't an option in his mind.

Chapter Nine

"Would you bring me another beer?" Quade asked from his position on the patio.

"I thought you might ask," Kai chuckled. He set the snack tray down on the small table and handed Quade a fresh bottle of beer.

"I still can't believe this place," Quade grumbled. "No wonder Cattle Valley seemed like hell to you."

Kai took his normal spot on Quade's lap and looked out over the ocean. His home wasn't fancy or large, but it had one of the best views on Oahu. "It serves as a reminder," he mused.

"Of what, babe?" Quade asked, rubbing Kai's stomach.

"Not to devote my entire life to surfing."

Quade chuckled. "Yeah, I can see that. You sit here looking out at the water and are reminded not to devote too much time to it," Quade joked.

Kai shook his head. "It's not that. This place was built by my friend, Mano. He's the man who taught

me to surf. I was around eight when I first met him."
Kai pointed towards the beach. "Right out there,
actually."

He could still picture it clearly. Mano stood in the
water up to his knees, looking out at the ocean. With
his waist-length hair blowing in the wind, Kai had
thought him some kind of Hawaiian god.

"He'd been a professional surfer, like me, and had
done well enough to buy this place," Kai gestured to
the surroundings.

"Problem was, he'd spent so much time and energy
in the ocean, Mano didn't know how to relate to
people on dry land. But he was my friend. My dad
was always out on deployment, so Mano became like
a surrogate father to me." Kai had silently wished
Mano was his real dad, but he'd never told anyone
that.

"I used to ask him why he didn't have a wife and
kids. He'd usually brush me off, but once, when I was
around sixteen, he told me he'd lost the love of his life
because he'd put surfing first."

Kai wrapped his arms around Quade's neck and
kissed him. "Mano told me nothing was worth
growing old alone. He made me promise to treat
surfing like a job and not my life." Kai shrugged.
"When he died six years ago, he left me this place. So
now, when I sit and stare out at the water, I think
about him, and I remember."

Quade was silent for several moments. "You'll never
leave it, will you?"

"I'll never sell it, no. But I'm not dead-set on living
in it for the rest of my life either." Kai turned to
straddle Quade's lap. He gazed deep into the eyes of

the man he loved. "I'm sorry I left you. Sometimes I wonder if I'm cursed to end up like Mano, old and lonely."

"Not if I have any say in it," Quade declared.

"I wish I could fit into your world. Move to Cattle Valley and get a job, but I can't. I barely finished high school. Surfing is all I know."

Quade ran his fingers down the side of Kai's face. "What happens after the tournaments stop? What'll you do then?"

Kai had thought of that very thing many times. He'd never shared his ideas with anyone. If he didn't become world champion they wouldn't mean much anyway. "Promise you won't laugh?"

Quade actually looked hurt at the question. "I'd never laugh at you."

Kai jumped off of Quade's lap and went to the spare bedroom. Opening the closet, he pulled out the giant sketchpad. He hugged the well-used pad to his chest. *Please don't make fun of me*, he prayed.

Taking the sketches out to the patio, he handed them to Quade. "No one else knows about this."

With a questioning look, Quade took the binder and opened it. Kai bit his lip as he watched Quade flip from one sketch to the next. "I don't know if it'll work. I mean, I haven't built a prototype or anything," he defended, looking at the surfboards he'd designed.

"These are incredible."

"Really?" Kai smiled. "Of course they'll just gather dust if I can't make a name for myself on the circuit. No one will take a chance on a newly designed board from a nobody. But if I can win..."

"You'll have a name to attach to the new concept," Quade finished for him.

"And the money," Kai added.

Quade nodded and set the sketches aside. He pulled Kai back into his lap and sighed heavily. "You need to be here for that dream to work."

Kai knew what his lover was saying. Quade was right. Kai would never be able to move to Cattle Valley. Who would buy a surfboard made in Wyoming? He rested his cheek against the top of Quade's head. "We'll figure something out," he mumbled.

* * * *

Turning the page of his book, Quade's gaze drifted towards the ocean. He'd spent his entire first week on the island trying to figure out how to make a life with Kai work. When he'd realised his hopes of Kai retiring after a couple of years and moving to Cattle Valley wasn't going to happen, he'd been crushed.

The fact that his lover came home nightly with a new set of bruises didn't help matters. He was worried that Van's brand of training would be the death of his young lover, but nothing he said seemed to make a difference. Kai was determined to soak up Van's knowledge like a sponge.

Quade's curiosity had gotten the better of him, and he'd looked Van Duggins up on the internet earlier that morning. What he found worried him even more. It was no wonder Van hadn't picked another surfer to train in almost ten years. Quade wondered if Kai knew about his mentor's past?

"Thought I'd find you out here," Kai said, coming up behind Quade's chair.

Tilting his head back, Quade looked up at his lover. "Good day?"

"Okay." Kai grinned. "No fresh booboos for you to kiss."

"Oh, well then, I'll just have to kiss the old ones," Quade chuckled, standing to pull Kai into his arms. He closed the distance and drew Kai into a deep kiss. Quade wondered if he'd ever get tired of kissing this man.

Running his hands down Kai's muscled back, Quade slipped them under the waistband of his lover's board shorts. "Mmmm," he moaned, sliding his fingers down the sandy crack of Kai's ass. "Someone needs a shower," he commented, breaking the kiss.

"Someone needs you more."

"We could compromise and shower together," Quade groaned, reaching around to cup Kai's balls.

"Sounds like a plan," Kai agreed, diving back in for another kiss.

Quade broke the kiss and buried his face in Kai's hair. Inhaling, he smiled. His lover always smelled like sunshine and salt water. How would he survive even a day without that smell?

Kai stepped back and tugged Quade's hand out of his swim trunks. "Shower," he reminded Quade. "The sooner all my bits are clean, the sooner I can impale myself."

Quade let Kai lead him into the house, shedding clothes as they went. "I talked to Nate earlier. Cattle Valley's hunkering down for another blizzard. That's two already this year."

"Bet you're glad you're here," Kai commented, turning on the water.

"Yeah," Quade said, looking at the sweet curve of Kai's bare ass. "I feel kinda bad for Carol though. In a town the size of Cattle Valley it's usually up to me to coordinate the clean-up between the road crew, electricity company, sanitation department..." Quade exhaled. "The list goes on and on."

Kai turned, tilting his head to the side. "You love it, don't you?"

Did he? He usually spent all winter bitching about the added work, but in that moment Quade realised he did indeed love it. "Yeah, I do. I honestly can't imagine doing anything else."

After several quiet moments, Quade gave his head a slight shake. "Water warm?"

Kai spun around and stepped into the shower. "Yep. Coming in?"

"You bet your sweet ass," Quade replied, and removed the rest of his clothing. Before entering, he took the time to study his lover. "Christ. You really are amazing," he whispered.

Kai pulled his head out from under the spray. "Huh? Did you say something?" he asked, reaching for the shampoo.

Quade grinned. "I said don't hog all the water." He slipped inside and closed the glass door, as the younger man took a step back.

Kai handed Quade a bottle of shower gel. "Feel up to washing my bits?"

Quade took the bottle and poured some of the sporty fragranced soap into his hand. He started with Kai's chest, feeling the dark brown nipples pebble under his touch. The expression on Kai's face when Quade's hands roamed south was one of love and need. He wondered if his face showed the desperation he felt, not only for Kai's body, but for his heart as well?

Quade spun Kai to face the tiled wall. He pressed himself against the warm curves of his lover and hoped his insecurities hadn't been on display. After obtaining a fresh supply of gel, Quade sunk to his knees. "Your ass is incredible," he groaned, sliding his slick hands over and between Kai's butt cheeks.

Kai braced his arms against the wall and spread his legs. "Kiss me," Kai begged.

Quade knew what his lover wanted. With a hand on each cheek, Quade spread Kai open to the spray of water, removing soap and sand. He buried his face, twirling his tongue around the ridged opening. How many times had he fucked this ass in the previous week?

As Quade pushed his tongue inside Kai's heat, he knew it didn't matter. He was well and truly addicted. The big question was what would the withdrawals do to him?

"Fuck me," Kai panted, lifting his foot to rest on the soap alcove.

"Squirt some gel into my hand," Quade commanded.

Kai's body accepted Quade's fingers easily. No surprise there. Hell, the two of them couldn't be together without fucking. Within a few minutes, Kai was stretched and moaning. Quade stood and positioned his cock. "You ready for me?" he teased, inserting his crown before withdrawing it.

Kai tilted his head back to land on Quade's shoulder. "Give it to me."

With his hands on Kai's waist, Quade grunted. "Put both feet up. I won't drop ya."

Kai rewarded him with a trusting nod as he put his other foot in the niche cut into the wall. Pressing the head of his cock past the outer ring of muscles, Quade used his hands to stabilise Kai. "It's all yours," Quade began. "Show me just how hungry that sweet little ass is."

With a loud groan, Kai impaled himself on the entire length of Quade's cock. "Fuck!" Quade yelled at the almost spontaneous envelopment. He tightened his grip on Kai's narrow hips as his lover used his footholds to fuck himself with Quade's dick.

Quade's eyes roamed Kai's powerful back muscles as they danced and twitched. Never had a lover's body been more perfectly matched to Quade's desires.

"You sure you got me? Cuz I'm gonna let go," Kai panted, picking up his pace.

"I'll always have you, babe," Quade answered.

With a breathless chuckle, Kai fisted his cock with one hand, while the other reached behind Quade to pull him in for a kiss. Quade opened to accept his lover's tongue as it slid deep into his mouth.

Despite the water temperature dropping dramatically, Quade's forehead broke out into a sweat at the erotic scene reflected in the mirror over the sink. "Love you," Quade declared. "No matter what happens, I need you to remember that."

Kai's body jerked in his arms, the younger man crying out as his orgasm overtook him. Knowing Kai was satisfied, Quade allowed himself to let go, his seed shooting in long spurts deep into his lover's body. He felt his knees begin to tremble at the intensity of his climax and lowered Kai to the floor.

As the cool water rained down on their overheated bodies, Quade held Kai in his arms. Quade knew if he lost Kai, he'd never love again. It may not last forever, but he was determined to do right by the trusting, younger man.

* * * *

Kai woke to the sound of rattling dishes. Opening his eyes, he watched as Quade set the table. "You cooked?"

Quade jumped, almost upsetting the wineglass and turned around. "You're up?" The older man glanced back at the table. "Yeah, I thought I'd fix a little pasta. Hungry?"

Yawning, Kai ran his hand down his naked torso to scratch his balls. "Starved." He swung his legs over the side of the couch and sat up. "I'm sorry. I can't believe I just crashed like that."

"Must've been a hell of a workout," Quade commented, setting several bowls onto the table.

"It was." Kai stood and stretched. "I can't believe how much I've been doing wrong. It's amazing I've gotten as far as I have."

He heard Quade huff a sound of disagreement before quickly covering it with a cough. "What?" Kai asked. "Something bothering you?"

It took several moments, but Quade eventually pulled out a chair and sat down. "Come here." He held out his arms and waited for Kai to join him.

Uh oh. Kai grabbed his robe from the chair and shrugged into it. "What's going on?" he asked, sitting on Quade's lap.

Quade smoothed the short silk robe over Kai's thighs. "I know you think Van is wonderful, but I did some research and found something disturbing."

About Van? Wait a minute. That's beside the point. "Why were you checking up on Van?"

Quade shrugged. "Jealousy. After I met him, I needed to know something about the gorgeous guy who was spending long days with you."

Kai rolled his eyes. Van's apparent indifference towards Kai when they were together was definitely not a secret. "Some days I don't think the guy even likes me as a student. You don't need to worry about him trying to get into my pants."

Shifting, Kai straddled Quade's lap. "I love you. If all I wanted was to get laid, I could sure as hell find someone younger than Van."

Quade narrowed his eyes. "I'm gonna pretend you didn't just make a crack about the guy's age."

"All I'm saying is…I don't want anyone but you."

Quade gave a subtle nod. "Did you know his last protégé was killed during a tournament?"

"Sure. Everyone in the surfing community knows what happened to Blain Hardesty."

"So you know that he was trying to execute a manoeuvre Van had perfected when he won the championship years earlier? That the judges interviewed said Blain was in no way ready to perform such a manoeuvre?"

Kai gave Quade's chest a push and tried to stand. Quade's muscular arms tightened around him, preventing his escape. "Yeah, I know all that. Did your little research trip tell you the two of them were lovers? That Van completely shut down after Blain's death? Or that Van held Blain's body as he took his last breath?"

Quade's face paled. "No," he had the decency to admit.

"What about the fact that Blain's brother Bryan was there too. That Bryan and I had been lovers at the time, so we were both there cheering Blain on?"

Kai closed his eyes and rested his head against Quade's shoulder. "That tragedy ruined so many people's lives." He sat back and gazed into Quade's eyes. "I'm not Blain. He was a selfish, conceited prick who used Van to get ahead. I'm not like that."

"I know you're not," Quade added. "I fucked up. I'm sorry. I was worried."

"Don't be." Kai leaned forward and placed a soft kiss on Quade's lips. "Surfers always make the comment that if they're going to bite it, they want it to be in the water." Kai shook his head. "Not me. I've seen what it does to the people left on land. I listen to what Van teaches me because he knows what the hell he's talking about. Blain's accident wasn't Van's fault."

Quade crushed Kai against his chest. "I can't lose you. I'm not sure how deep Van's feelings were for Blain, but it would kill me if you got hurt."

Kai knew he'd overreacted. The mention of Blain brought up too many bad memories. Brian had been Kai's first lover, and he fancied himself in love. The tragedy destroyed anything that might've been between him and Brian. His young lover had snapped.

Brian sank into such a pit of anger and depression, his family eventually admitted him into a psych ward.

Yeah, he'd definitely seen first-hand what dying on a board did to the survivors. "I won't ever do something out there that isn't safe. I promise."

Quade tilted Kai's chin to face him. "That's all I can ask." He gave Kai a deep kiss. "Our dinner's getting cold."

Kai grinned. "Can't have that. I'm a growing boy."

Quade reached between them and ran his hand over the length of Kai's cock. "In more ways than one."

Chapter Ten

"Okay, I just sent it," Quade said, phone to his ear. "Tell Ryan to give Guy Hoisington the heads-up that Brewster's is under new ownership."

"I still can't believe that asshole got away with everything," Carol fumed.

"We couldn't very well prosecute him without going after David. Guy made it perfectly clear to the prosecuting attorney all he wanted was restitution for the damage done to The Tall Pines." Quade moved Kai's keyboard to the side of the desk and put his feet up. "So what else is goin' on?"

"Um, let me think. Snow, snow and more snow, jackass," Carol chuckled.

Quade looked out the window to the bright sunny day. "I hear ya. It's chilly here today as well. I think it's down to eighty degrees."

"Fuck off."

Smiling, Quade thought of Kai. "Okay I can do that. It's time to pick Kai up anyway. Call if you need anything else."

"I miss you, you turd. Things just aren't the same without you around bugging the shit out of me."

Quade made a smooching sound into the phone. "I love you too. I'll be back on Monday."

"I'll alert the press," Carol joked.

Quade hung up the phone and got to his feet. He couldn't believe he only had three days left to be with Kai. What would it be like to wake without that sweet mouth wrapped around his morning wood?

Thinking about their morning ritual, Quade's cock began to fill. "Not yet," he crooned, petting the front of his shorts.

After grabbing Kai's keys from the coffee table, Quade roared out of the driveway. He always made it a point to leave at least an hour early so he could watch his lover in action. Quade hadn't had any more run-ins with Van, but the two of them did their best to keep their distance from each other.

Quade knew Van didn't approve of Kai getting into a serious relationship. Although Kai hadn't said anything about Van giving him a hard time, the younger man sure hustled Quade off the beach as soon as the lesson was over.

Finding a spot to park wasn't easy, but Quade managed one a quarter of a mile down the beach. By the time he found Kai and Van, he only had twenty minutes to watch his lover surf.

Trying to stay far enough away in order not to distract the lesson, Quade settled in the sand. Kai was on his board paddling his way out to catch a wave as Van looked on from his position on the beach, barking orders.

Quade had seen a remarkable change in Kai's style over the previous ten days. Quade knew his lover's ranking would rise dramatically after the first tournament in Australia. What he didn't know was how many seasons Kai would have to maintain his ranking in order to make the surf board manufacturing dream viable.

Just when Kai caught a wave, Quade's cell phone rang. He thought about ignoring it in favour of the view, but his conscience got the better of him. Digging the phone out of his short's pocket, he looked at the display. Shit. Quade's thumb hovered over the button for two more rings. With a resigned sigh, he pressed the key. "Hi, Mother."

"Hello, dear. I need you to come home. The doctor admitted your father into the hospital this morning."

Quade sat up and brushed the sand from his torso. "What's wrong?"

"Nelson hasn't been feeling well so Dr. Thrumbolt gave him a complete physical. Nelson's blood pressure is elevated and he didn't do well with the stress test. The doctor thought it would be best to admit your father for further testing."

"He's a businessman, Mother. Of course his blood pressure is high. Father probably wouldn't be able to function at the pace he does if it wasn't," Quade quipped.

"Nelson Quade Madison, I'm surprised at you. Your father has sacrificed everything for his family. The least you can do is pay your respects by coming back to Charleston."

Quade bit his tongue. His father didn't sacrifice anything for his family. Nelson Madison was a cheating son-of-a-bitch, who thought nothing of his wife and child. It had always been that way. More than once his dad had missed an important family event due to work or his mistress-of-the-month. Quade knew it, and he was certain his mother also knew it, but it wouldn't fit into Lorraine Madison's views on social niceties. Instead his mother looked the other way, giving Nelson free reign.

"Dear?" Lorraine prompted.

"I'm in Hawaii, Mother."

"So, it will take you a little longer to get to Charleston. When can I expect you?"

"We don't even know what's wrong. Why don't you let me know if the doctor finds something, and I'll consider flying back then?"

"Because I need you here, now, that's why. There are things that need looking after in your father's absence, business things. We both know he would expect you to take care of Madison Industries."

"Why are you talking about him like he's already dead? Hell, Mother, by the time I get there, he could be out of the hospital and back to work."

"Not this time," Lorraine said.

"What aren't you telling me?" Quade's gaze landed on Kai as he stood on the beach talking to Van.

"There's something to do with his white blood cell count. I'm not sure what it means, but Dr. Thrumbolt didn't seem pleased."

Quade knew an elevated white cell count usually signalled an infection of some kind, but was it enough to drag him away from the man he loved? That was the big question. His father had always been aloof, more interested in his own business and social life.

Quade couldn't remember a time when Nelson's family had ever come first.

"I'll think about it," he finally said.

"Please, son," his mom pleaded.

How many times had he held his mother's hand after one of his father's affairs had come to light? "I said I'd think about it and I will. Call if Dr. Thrumbolt finds something."

Lorraine sighed dramatically. "I can't believe you're being so selfish about this."

"I learned from the best. Talk to you later, Mother."

Kai started towards him, and Quade ended the call. Shoving the phone back into his pocket, he stood and met his lover halfway. "You looked good out there," he said, greeting Kai with a kiss.

"Thanks," Kai said, pressing further against Quade.

Chuckling, Quade pulled back and looked down at his now wet shorts. "People are gonna talk," he joked.

"Let them." Kai nibbled Quade's lower lip before soothing the sting with his tongue. "Who were you talking to?"

"My mother," Quade divulged, running his hands down Kai's back to land on his ass. "My father's in the hospital. She wants me to fly to Charleston."

"Is he going to be okay?" Kai asked with a note of concern.

Quade shrugged. "Who knows. Maybe his fast paced life finally caught up with him."

He released his hold on Kai and pulled his lover's board from the sand, settling it under his arm. "Ready to go?"

"Yeah," Kai said, following. "So, uh, you gonna go?"

Quade manoeuvred the board around several people before answering. "Not sure. I told her to call me if the doctor found anything."

"You never talk about your parents," Kai mused.

"Not much to talk about. They weren't around much while I was growing up. Hell, I think my nanny loved me more than either of them ever did."

"What was her name?" Kai asked.

"Gloria," Quade said after a few moments. "She was the kind of woman every child wished was their grandmother. Gloria was the one to pick me up from school, take me to the park, and tuck me in at night while my parents went to whatever social engagement was more important."

Talking about the older woman caused a hitch in Quade's breathing. "She had a massive stroke when I was around thirteen. I remember getting worried when she didn't pick me up from school. I called home but no one answered. Then I called my father's office. He yelled at me. Told me to take the bus and stop acting like a pussy."

They arrived at Kai's Jeep, and Quade loaded the bright yellow and red board into the back. "By the time I got home, Gloria was dead. I found her on the kitchen floor with a grocery list still in her hand." Quade shrugged and got behind the wheel. "After her funeral my parents informed me that I was old enough to take care of myself, so I did."

Kai's lips whispered across Quade's jaw. "I'm sorry. I can tell you loved her."

"Yeah," Quade sighed. "She was probably the only person I've ever loved besides you."

"And that's why you're afraid something will happen to me," Kai said, finishing Quade's thought.

Quade realised Kai was right. "Yeah, I guess so."

He pulled out of the parking space and headed the jeep to Kai's house. "So, what do you feel like for dinner?" he asked, quickly changing the subject.

* * * *

Kai set the plate of seafood leftovers by the side of the house. He had no doubt the neighbourhood stray cat would be by within minutes to eat up the tasty offering. Before rejoining Quade, Kai wandered down to the beach.

They had talked over dinner, and Kai was pretty sure Quade would do as his mother had asked and fly to Charleston. Kai knew Quade was doing the right thing, but it didn't make saying goodbye any easier.

Warm arms wrapped around his chest. "Beautiful sunset," Quade murmured.

Kai had been so lost in thought he hadn't even noticed the bright coloured blazes in the sky as the sun slowly dipped into the ocean. "It is," he agreed.

Quade sat down and pulled Kai into his lap. "Care to share it with me?"

Kai had seen thousands of Hawaiian sunsets. He chose instead to nestle against Quade's strong chest and look at his lover's face. How long would it be before they could be together again? "I'm gonna miss you," he blurted.

Quade's gaze drifted from the view down to Kai. "Me too. You have no idea how much."

"Maybe I can skip a tournament or two and make another trip to Cattle Valley?" Kai slipped his hand under Quade's unbuttoned shirt to run across his lover's chest. The days Quade had spent lounging on the beach had turned the skin under Kai's fingers a light golden brown colour.

Quade's hand covered Kai's, stilling his wandering touch. "We both know that you can't do that and still maintain your rankings." Quade closed the distance and swept his tongue through the interior of Kai's mouth. "We'll find a way. Hell, I've never been to half the places you're going this season. Maybe I'll sneak away and join you in Fiji or Australia."

"What time is your flight?" Kai asked.

Instead of answering, Quade stood with Kai still in his arms. "I've got fourteen hours left to worship this beautiful body of yours."

Kai nodded. He could still see the last glimmer of the setting sun around Quade's shoulder. "I called Van and told him I'd be taking you to the airport. He said it would probably be better to skip practice all together. That I'd be distracted."

Quade carried him into the cool interior of the house, through to Kai's bedroom. "Promise me you won't let anything distract you from staying safe? The two of us will be together somehow, but you worrying about it can be dangerous."

Kai grinned. "Now you sound like Van." He pushed his shorts and underwear down over his hips and stepped out of them.

Quade stripped out of his clothes and pulled Kai down on the bed. "I've been keeping a close eye on that guy. Despite the rough way he talks to you, I think he does indeed have your safety in mind. Listen to him."

"I will." Kai ran his foot up the strong muscled thigh to wrap around Quade's lower back. Having Quade's full weight on top of him made him feel more loved and protected than anything else.

The two of them had made love so many times over the previous month, Kai didn't even need to ask for what he wanted. Quade picked up on Kai's body language and reached for the lube on the nightstand.

The insertion of Quade's fingers caused gooseflesh to pop out on Kai's skin. "Promise me we won't drift apart," he blurted when Quade introduced a second finger.

"Never," Quade vowed, exchanging his fingers for the crown of his cock. "You're mine, and I'll do everything in my power to keep it that way."

Kai's head pressed deeper into the pillow as Quade slowly entered him. He liked hearing Quade refer to him as his. "Love you," he moaned, accepting Quade's full length.

Quade rose to his hands and looked down at Kai. "You're everything to me. Remember that."

Quade pulled out and surged back inside, somehow getting even deeper. Kai watched the twin veins in his lover's neck pulse as the rhythm increased. Hitching his legs even higher on Quade's back, Kai turned every ounce of control over to the wonderful man making love to him.

"Mark me," he gasped, needing something to remind him of Quade after his lover left.

Quade's mouth latched on to a portion of skin above Kai's heart. The faster Quade's hips pistoned as he drove himself in and out of Kai's body, the harder he sucked.

"Ooohh," Kai moaned, feeling the bruise raise on his chest.

Quade groaned as he pulled his mouth from Kai's skin and gazed down at his handiwork. "Roll to your side," Quade grunted, plunging deep once more before withdrawing completely.

Kai did as asked and waited for Quade to spoon against his back into their favourite morning position. *Why like this? Why now?*

After applying more lube to his cock, Quade re-entered Kai in one thrust. He curled his body around Kai's and buried his face in Kai's neck. "I'm not gonna make it," Quade choked, slowly moving in and out of Kai's body.

"That's okay. We've got all night," Kai answered, turning his head to steal a kiss.

Quade slowly shook his head. "I mean I'm not gonna make it without you in my arms every day."

It was then he noticed the tears running down Quade's cheeks. "Shhh," Kai soothed. "This isn't the end. We'll figure it out."

Kai turned his face into the pillow, trying to believe his own words. He knew how much Quade loved his little Utopian town. Was building surf boards more important than being with the man he loved? Hell, for that matter, was surfing worth it?

Quade's thumb rubbed against the new bruise on Kai's chest as the intensity of their coupling became almost frenzied. Kai pushed back onto Quade's cock. "Fuck me," he begged, wrapping his hand around his own shaft.

Fucking him like a man possessed, Quade opened Kai further with a forearm under his knee. "Don't. Want. It. To. End," Quade punctuated each word with a deep thrust.

"It won't." Kai believed that, he had to. Giving up the man he loved wasn't an option.

Chapter Eleven

Quade was already out of sorts when he arrived at the hospital after a twenty hour day. The long plane ride combined with hours spent lurking around airports waiting for connecting flights had given him too much time to think.

"It's about time," his mother greeted sarcastically, as Quade walked into his father's room.

Quade stopped and dropped his luggage just inside the doorway. "Do you have any idea how far I've travelled, Mother?"

Dismissing the disapproving glare, Quade turned his attention to the bed. "How is he?" he asked, walking over to look down at his sleeping father.

"They have him scheduled for an angioplasty in the morning. Dr. Thrumbolt thinks the years of stress have finally caught up with your father."

Quade noticed his mother never rose from her chair in the corner of the room. He wondered if she'd even held his father's hand since he'd been admitted. Was she here out of duty, or love? He knew he was there strictly out of duty. His father had never been around enough for Quade to form a real bond with the man. "What do you need me to do?" he finally asked.

"I can take care of things here, if you'll make sure the office is still running. Those people probably think they're on vacation without your father around. Make sure they know it's business as usual."

Business as usual? "I don't know the first thing about running Madison Industries."

"Well it's time you learned. Your father has spent his entire life breathing life back into that company after your granddad nearly lost everything."

Unconsciously, Quade began grinding his teeth. It was an old argument, one he didn't care to have at the moment. "I'm going back to the house to grab a nap and a shower. I'll head into the office later if there's still time."

"You should at least call the office. It wouldn't hurt to let them know you could pop in at any moment."

Quade rolled his eyes, refusing to answer her request. He gave his father one last glance before walking over to pick up his luggage. "Will my key still work in the lock?"

"No," Lorraine stated. "The housekeeper will need to let you in."

Quade looked at the keyring in his hand. He'd been carrying around five extra keys for years for nothing? "Why'd you change the locks?"

Lorraine looked at him like he was crazy. "Because you moved out."

"What? Why? Did you think I was going to break in and steal something? Jesus, Mother!"

Crossing her arms over her chest, Lorraine's chin lifted. "You're the one who left."

Deciding it wasn't worth the argument, Quade shouldered his carry-on and flung open the door. "Call me on my cell if there are any changes."

* * * *

With a towel around his waist, Quade sat on the guest bed and called Kai. The completely redesigned bedroom said a lot about his relationship with his parents. He briefly wondered how long they'd waited before packing all his boyhood stuff into storage.

When the call went directly to voice mail, Quade sighed. "Hi. I just wanted you to know I finally made it. I'm getting ready to lie down. Call me when you get in. Love you." Quade hung up and dropped his towel before sliding between the high thread-count taupe sheets.

He was turning over the idea of shirking his familial duties and flying back to Kai, when his phone rang. Reaching over to the ornately carved bedside table, Quade smiled when he looked at the display. "Hey, babe."

"Hi. How's your dad?" Kai asked.

"He'll be fine I guess. Mother didn't let me stay long at the hospital, so I thought I'd come back to the house and take a nap. How'd the training go?" Quade snuggled back under the covers with the phone tucked between his chin and shoulder.

He noticed Kai didn't answer his question. "Kai? Did something happen?"

"No. Well, not really. Had a pretty good wipe-out, but I'll be okay."

Quade's entire body tensed. "You'll be okay? How bad were you hurt?" He mentally calculated the time difference and how long it would take to get back to Oahu.

"Relax. Just a few new bruises, nothing major. Although my ears are still ringing after Van chewed my ass for being so careless."

Quade could very well imagine the choice words Van would have used. "I'm glad he's looking out for your safety. How'd it happen?"

"I still don't know. I guess my head just wasn't in it."

The thought of his lover doing something to hurt himself almost sent Quade over the edge. "Were you thinking about us?"

"Of course. You're never far from my thoughts."

"Listen, babe. You have to promise me you'll be careful. I'm doing enough thinking and worrying for the both of us. You just concentrate on the wave and let me deal with the rest."

"I miss you already," Kai murmured.

"I miss you too." Quade ran his hand down under the covers. He gave his filling cock a quick stroke before wincing. "My dick's still sore," he chuckled, thinking about the hours they'd spent in bed before his departure.

"Yeah? You should feel my ass," Kai quipped.

"I'd love to feel your ass." Quade imagined his cock buried between the tight globes of Kai's ass.

Kai giggled. "Not today you wouldn't."

"Any day, any hour, any minute." Quade felt his breathing hitch in his chest as he tried to imagine the long weeks and months until he could be with Kai again.

"Mmmm. That sounds nice," Kai replied.

Quade yawned, the long trip catching up to him.

"Why don't you take your nap, and call me when you wake up," Kai said.

"By that time it'll be the middle of the night for you. I'll wait until you wake up in the morning."

"Love you," Kai whispered.

Quade drifted off to sleep with Kai's name still on his lips.

* * * *

Quade strode into the offices of Madison Industries after a fitful nap. How long had it been since he'd last walked through the heavy glass doors? Five years? Six? He stopped at the reception desk to introduce himself. "Hi, I'm Quade Madison. My mother asked me to stop by. Does Paul Quirk still work here?"

"Yes, Mr. Madison. Would you like me to call him for you?"

Quade shook his head. "I'll surprise him. Is he still in the same office?"

"I'm not sure where he used to be. I've only been with the company for a year, but you'll find Mr. Quirk in Suite four-sixteen."

"He's a Vice-President?" Quade asked, more than a little shocked. He'd gone to college with Paul and had helped him get the job in marketing when they'd both graduated.

"Yes, sir," the receptionist said, trying to ignore the incessantly ringing phones.

Quade tapped his palm on her desk. "I'll find him, thanks." He walked to the bank of elevators and pushed the up button. Paul a Vice-President? He still couldn't believe it. He wondered why his father had never mentioned promoting his old friend.

The doors opened and Quade stepped inside along with a few other employees, none of whom he recognised. He was a little ashamed of himself for going so long between visits. There was a time when he'd roam the halls of Madison Industries at least once a week. Of course it was the only way he saw his father.

Stepping off the elevator onto the executive floor, Quade nodded to a few familiar faces as he made his way to Paul's office. "Is he in?" Quade asked the secretary, sitting outside Paul's door.

"Is he expecting you?" the cute little blonde asked.

"No. I'm Quade Madison. Paul and I went to college together." He started to walk towards his friend's door, but the woman stopped him.

"I'm sorry, Mr. Madison, but Paul likes everyone to be announced in case he's in the middle of something."

"Oh. Okay." Quade waited while the secretary did her job.

"You can go in," she said, hanging up the phone.

With a slight shake to his head, Quade opened the door. The man sitting behind the large desk was still as good-looking as Quade remembered. "Hey, Mr. Vice-President," he greeted.

"Quade, you old dog, what brings you to Charleston?" Paul stood and shook Quade's hand.

"Mother asked me to come. My father's in the hospital," he divulged, not surprised that his father's employees knew nothing of his health. With Nelson Madison, it was all about work. Nothing else was worth discussing.

"Nelson's okay, I hope," Paul said, motioning Quade to sit.

Settling in the black leather and chrome chair, Quade nodded. "He should be fine in a day or two."

Quade glanced around Paul's office. "I can't believe you're one of those muckety-mucks we used to joke about in school."

Paul looked briefly offended. "I'm very good at my job."

"Of course you are. My father wouldn't have promoted you if you weren't the best. Just surprised me is all." Quade suddenly felt ill-at-ease. "So, what's been going on? You married?"

Paul scoffed and waved his hand. "Divorced. Twice actually. Wives require too much of my time. I'd rather exert my energy and attention here where it'll do me some good. What about you? You still living in that town out west?"

"Cattle Valley, yep. I'm Mayor Quade Madison to the people of the community," Quade boasted.

"Good for you. I guess there's no need to ask about a wife," Paul chuckled.

A picture of Kai came to mind. "My partner's name is Kai. He's a professional surfer living in Oahu at the moment."

Paul whistled. "Boy when you do it, you do it right. Maybe I should try a long-distance relationship. It'd be a lot easier to make time for phone calls during the day than trying to get home in time for dinner."

"Well, we're not long-distance by choice. Our jobs just happen to conflict with our living arrangements," Quade excused.

"I hear ya. People don't understand how important careers are to a man. Well worth giving up a nightly piece of ass for, wouldn't you say?" Paul laughed.

Quade wanted to shout NO! He looked at his friend, really looked at him for the first time. Paul appeared...old. Quade wondered if it was trying to keep up with Corporate America or the lack of someone to love. He thought of his father. Last time Quade had seen him his father looked much older than his sixty-two years.

"Listen," he said, standing. "I'll let you get back to work. I need to see if anything requires attention."

He said his goodbyes and left as fast as he could. Quade walked to the other end of the hall to his father's office.

"Quade!" Louise, his father's long-time secretary said, throwing her arms around him. "You're so handsome." The older woman stepped back to look him up and down.

"Aww, I bet you say that to all the boss' sons." He winced as Louise pinched his cheek.

"You still have that mouth on you I see?" Louise remarked, turning the pinch into a pat. "How's Nelson?"

"I'm not really sure to be honest. Mother hustled me out of the hospital quickly after I arrived. She said father was due to have an angioplasty performed in the morning." Quade sighed. "To be honest, I'm still not sure why she needed me to cut my vacation short and fly down here."

Louise tapped her chin and retook her chair behind the desk. "I've my own theory on that."

"Care to enlighten me?" Quade asked, leaning on the edge of the desk.

Louise's eyes scanned the surrounding area before speaking. "He's made no secret of wanting you to take over when he retires. The company has been run by a Madison for the past eighty years."

Quade shook his head. "I've told him a million times I wanted nothing to do with the company."

Louise nodded her head sympathetically. "He's getting older, Quade. I think he realises he didn't do right by you when you were growing up. He wants you here with him so he can teach you what he should have taught you years ago."

"It's too late," Quade ground out. "Family business or not, I would never have put this place above spending time with the people I loved."

Quade had to brace himself against the desk as the words sank in. *Fuck! I'm doing the same thing. Only instead of depriving a son, I'm depriving the man I love.*

Pounding his fist against the cold surface, he stood. "Sorry, Louise, but I need to go."

"Is there something wrong?"

"Yeah," Quade realised. "But now that I know what it is, I can make it right." He leaned over and gave the older woman a kiss on the cheek. "Take care of yourself. Don't let them work you too hard."

"Pssh," Louise waved him off. "I wouldn't still be here if I let these barracudas get to me."

Quade ran out of the building, eager to set in motion the path that would lead to his happiness.

* * * *

Suitcases in hand, Quade entered his father's hospital room. "How is he?" he asked.

Lorraine glanced up from a fashion magazine, before returning to whatever article she happened to be reading. "He's awake. Aren't you, Nelson?"

Nelson Madison's eyes opened to stare at his son. "How're things at the office?"

Quade sighed, knowing it was too much for his father to greet him properly. "Fine, I guess. Aren't you going to ask how I've been?"

"No problems with the Henderson account?"

Why do I even bother? "None that I heard about."

Quade watched as his father's lids closed once more, obviously dismissing his only son. "I'm leaving," Quade declared.

Nelson's eyes shot back open. "What? You can't. I'll be in here at least another couple of days. You need to keep an eye on the office, report back to me."

Scrubbing his hands over his tired eyes, Quade kicked himself for giving these people any of his precious time. "I don't give a fuck about Madison Industries. I'm going home to Cattle Valley. There are a few things I need to take care of before moving to Oahu."

"Oahu? What the hell has you abandoning your responsibilities to move half-way across the globe?"

Squaring his shoulders, Quade looked his father in the eyes. "The man I love."

Nelson's face turned red as a beet. "I didn't work my entire life to have you shirking your duties to run after some queer boy."

Leaning over the bed, Quade grabbed the lapels of his father's blue-striped pyjamas. "You watch your mouth, you selfish sonofabitch."

"Quade!" Lorraine gasped, putting her hand to her chest. "What has gotten into you?"

Quade released his father and gazed at his mother. How many years had he prayed, hoping that someday his parents would love him? "Love, Mother. For the first time in my life someone truly loves me."

"Love doesn't pay the bills," his father broke in.

"How the hell would you know? Have you ever actually loved someone, or do you just equate love with a quick fuck over your lunch hour?"

Nelson flinched as Lorraine let out another loud gasp. Rolling his eyes, Quade looked at his mother. "Don't play the innocent, Mother, it doesn't suit you."

He walked over to the door and picked up his luggage. "You're two of the most self-centred people I've ever met. I ought to hate you both for the way you did or didn't raise me, but I don't. The fact is I really don't feel much of anything for either of you. But I do need to thank you. Coming here has cleared up a lot of questions. I know now that if I let my job interfere with my love life, a job is all I'll ever have."

Quade opened the door and glanced back over his shoulder. "I hope your procedure goes well, Father. I'll be in touch."

Leaving the hospital room, Quade felt as though a weight had been lifted from his shoulders. He was thirty-eight-years old. It was about time he followed a new path in life.

Chapter Twelve

Quade heard the door to the outer office open and close. "Carol?"

His secretary's head popped around the door jamb to his office. "Quade? What're you doing back so early?"

"Getting stuff cleaned up. Would you mind grabbing us a cup of coffee and coming in for a visit?"

"Sure," Carol answered, suspicion lacing her voice.

Quade heard the rustle of fabric as she took off her coat, hat and scarf. "Do you already have coffee brewing in there, or should I make a pot?" she asked.

"Got some, but it's almost gone." While Carol fussed around in her office, Quade continued to work. He took a new folder out of the box next to him on the floor and added a label.

Carol walked in with a cup in one hand and a pitcher of water in the other. "How long've you been here?" she asked, refilling his cup before making a new pot.

"Too long," Quade replied, tossing down his pen. He took a tentative sip of the hot beverage. "I've been trying to get some files in order."

Carol's steps faltered. "You? What's going on?"

"Have a seat."

Setting her cup on the edge of Quade's desk, Carol sat. "Are you dying?"

Quade began to chuckle. Leave it to Carol to come right out with it. "No, but I'm leaving."

"What do you mean you're leaving? You just got back."

Quade took a deep breath. He knew talking to his old friend would be the hardest part of the transition. He set his own cup on the desk and leaned forward, looking Carol in the eyes. "I'm stepping down as mayor and moving to Hawaii."

Carol sat up straighter in her chair, her eyes as big as an owl's. "Wow! I...I don't know what to say. I can't imagine this town without you."

"I know it's sudden," Quade began.

"Don't," Carol interrupted. "You don't have to explain yourself to me. I know how much you love that boy. It's just a shock."

Carol reached across the desk and squeezed Quade's hand. "What do you need me to do?"

Quade couldn't believe his friend was taking the news so well. He'd had visions of her screaming at him, telling him he was crazy, but she seemed fine with it. Unless... "What's going on? Why're you so calm?"

Carol sighed and released his hand. "Because I've seen it coming. Once upon a time, this job, this town, meant everything to you. That was until your vacation last year."

She shrugged. "You came back different. I tried to tell myself it was just your dick talking, but as the months wore on and you showed no interest in any other men, I knew."

"That I was in love," Quade contributed.

"Yes. Seeing Kai here…" She shook her head. "Well, the man was literally a fish out of water."

Quade felt warmth invade him. Despite all their petty arguments, Carol was the best friend a man could have. She understood him. "So you'll help me? I need to get the office in order."

"We'll need to schedule a council meeting to discuss a replacement," Carol added.

"Yep. And I'll need to get my house up for sale." There were so many things to do before he could join Kai again. "How're we gonna get it all done and still run the city?"

Carol stood, rolling her eyes. "I'm actually a lot more efficient than I've ever let on. I can deal with the day to day things as well as get your desk sorted."

She picked up her coffee cup and took a sip. "You're going to be busy trying to explain to your friends why you're leaving." Carol turned to leave, but stopped before she left Quade's office. "It's okay, you know. I'd do just about anything to find that special someone or someones as the case may be."

"You will." In his weaker, drunker moments, he'd complimented Carol on her curvaceous figure and long auburn hair. Of course as soon as he'd sobered, he'd denied ever having the conversations. The woman was too damn strong-minded as it was. The last thing he needed was to put up with a conceited secretary.

He wished others could see past her brash personality to the sensual woman he knew was hidden underneath. Unlike most of the women in Cattle Valley, Carol wasn't a lesbian. She'd moved to town with two men, who subsequently decided they'd be better without a woman in the middle. Quade had met her only briefly before the affair ended, but he knew enough about her, to see the change the betrayal caused.

"From your lips to God's ears," she called from her office.

Quade's eyes began to sting as they filled with tears. Maybe paperwork wasn't the only thing he needed to take care of before he left.

* * * *

"You look like shit," Van muttered in mid-stretch.

"Thanks," Kai snorted. He felt like shit.

Van stopped exercising and put his hands on his hips. "You trying to make yourself sick? You leave for the land down under in less than a week."

Kai looked at his mentor. Although showing weakness wasn't usually something he did, Kai dropped to the sand. "I'm a fucking mess. I can't eat. I can't sleep." He shook his head. "I live my entire day for a sixty-minute phone call."

Van mumbled something under his breath before sitting next to Kai. "What'll it take for you to get your head on straight? Because there's no way in hell you can surf in a tournament in this condition."

"I don't know," Kai confessed. "Maybe I can find a way to spend time with Quade between tournaments?"

"You won't get as much training in if you do."

"I know." He felt horrible for wasting Van's time. "So maybe I won't be as good as I could be, but I'll be happier. Shouldn't that count for something?"

Van's hand landed on Kai's shoulder. "In the sport of surfing? No. But in life?" Van seemed to ponder the answer for a few moments. "I think you'll be better off in the long run."

"You do?" Kai asked. Van was infamous for his work ethic. The man did nothing if it didn't involve surfing.

Van nodded. He picked up a handful of sand and let it fall through his fingers. "This? The beach, the ocean, it'll always be here, but it loses something when you don't have someone to enjoy it with."

Van shifted in the sand, clearly uncomfortable with the topic. "Competing is fantastic, but you'll always be a surfer, points and tournaments can't take that away from you. Take it from an old surfer, there needs to be more than that." Van grinned. "Loneliness sucks."

Kai couldn't help but to laugh. "I think that's the first time I've ever seen anything close to a smile on that handsome face of yours."

Van stood and brushed the sand from his hands. "Not much to smile about."

Before his mentor could walk off, Kai reached out and grabbed his hand. "Blain didn't deserve you."

Van shrugged. "Maybe not, but I deserve the guilt I carry for what happened."

"You didn't kill him."

"I didn't save him either." Van pulled his hand away and walked over to Kai's board. "You ready to do this?"

* * * *

Quade glanced around the table at the surprised faces. "So, that's that. We'll need to fill the mayoral position in the interim until we can hold a special election the first Tuesday in April."

The city council members still appeared to be in a state of shock. "I'd like to nominate George Manning." Quade looked across the table at the town's fire chief. "I know you have other duties, but with Carol still on staff, I think you'd have time for both."

A single black brow rose in response. "I'm not sure how well I could work with her. She doesn't seem to like me much."

Quade waved George's concerns away. "Don't take it personally. It's a self-defence thing she has going. Once you get to know her, you'll love her as much as I do."

George looked from Quade to the rest of the council. Quade was surprised by the blush blossoming on the tall man's cheeks. Was he embarrassed by the nomination, or was it something else? *Hmmm.*

"Winters are usually pretty slow at the firehouse. As much as I hate to see Quade leave town, I think I can step into the job for a few months. That is, if you all agree?"

"All those in favour of making George Manning interim mayor raise your hand?" Quade asked the council.

"Well, it looks unanimous," Quade declared. Watching as Asa Montgomery, Ryan Blackfeather, Palmer Wynfield, Pam Gleason, Jeb Baines, Sam Browning and Ryan Bronwyn lowered their hands.

Quade stood and reached across the conference table to shake George's hand. "Congratulations, Mr. Mayor."

George smiled and returned the handshake. "Who's gonna break the news to Carol?"

"I'll call her when I get home. Don't worry. You'll do fine."

Quade felt like jumping up and down with glee. Not only had he solved the major obstacle for his departure, but if he didn't miss his guess, he might have solved the problem of his lonely best friend as well. He sure as hell hoped he wasn't reading George's signals wrong. The man had always been pretty open about the fact he swung both ways, maybe Carol would get lucky and George would swing her way.

After the meeting, Ryan pulled Quade aside. "Care to have a drink before you head home?"

Quade looked at his watch. "Sure. Kai'll be training for another hour or two," he answered, following Ryan down the steps. "I'll follow you."

Starting his Escalade, Quade began to get nostalgic. The drive down Main Street brought to mind all the good times he'd had since moving to Cattle Valley. Maybe he could talk Kai into returning to the small town a couple of weeks a year. He smiled. He'd love to see Kai's face when the rodeo came to town.

Pulling up in front of Brewster's, Quade joined Ryan on the sidewalk. "Have you heard if the new owner is gonna change the name?" he asked, pointing at the bar sign.

Ryan chuckled and opened the front door. "With a name like Sean O'Brien I imagine the new owner will change more than the name. I think we might be in for a genuine Irish pub."

Quade laughed in return. "Yeah, I guess you're right." He gestured towards a booth. "Grab us a table while I get us the first round."

Ryan nodded and pulled out his cell phone. "I should probably call and tell the boys I'll be a little later than usual."

Quade grinned and walked towards the bar. The new owner was leaning against the scarred wood surface talking to Ben Zook. Quade had only met the man briefly when he'd returned from Charleston the previous week, but he hadn't forgotten him. The guy was pretty unforgettable. Quade imagined Sean must've been a professional body builder of some kind before moving to Cattle Valley. The man was huge, with a chest as wide as a barn. The slight red tint to his otherwise light brown hair would've given away Sean's heritage even if his name hadn't.

"Aahh, Mayor Madison," Sean greeted. "What can I get you?"

"Two bottles of Michelob, please." He decided not to tell anyone about his resignation until the formal announcement the following day.

As he waited, he looked around the bar. Was it busier than normal for a weeknight? He knew it probably had something to do with the new owner. Who could resist watching the muscles under the tight T-shirt dance as Sean worked?

The bottles landed in front of him and Quade pulled out a ten. "Keep the change."

Sean nodded. "Thanks."

Quade carried the bottles over to the booth and joined Ryan. "How long did the boys say you could stay out?" he asked.

Ryan grinned. "Well, when I told them the news, they decided to get dressed and join us. They should be here any time unless they get…distracted."

"The two of them? Naw," Quade joked. He took a sip of his beer and gazed at his friend. "I'm gonna miss you."

"You sure you're doing the right thing? What'll you do in Hawaii?"

"Fuck the man I love," Quade shot back before getting serious. "I'll find something to occupy my time. I've got enough money to travel with Kai for a couple of years. He's hoping to eventually open a surf and body board manufacturing shop. Just a small one, but I'm sure it'll be enough to keep us both busy."

"Does he know you're coming?"

Quade bit his bottom lip. "No. I'm worried that it'll throw off his concentration."

Ryan took a swig of his beer. "Surprises aren't always what they're cracked up to be. I think you should let him know you're coming at least. You don't have to tell him you're moving there if you don't want, but that's up to you."

Quade thought about it. "You may be right. I'll consider it."

Freezing cold hands covered Quade's eyes from behind before a pair of soft lips whispered against his ear. "I heard you think the scenery in Hawaii is prettier than here."

Quade grinned. Nate knew very well how pretty he was, but he was also very much taken. "Staring at the scenery in Hawaii won't get me killed," he answered back.

Laughing, Nate placed a kiss on Quade's neck before bumping him with his hip. "Scoot over."

Quade did as asked and wrapped his arm around Nate's neck, rubbing the man's perfect hair with his knuckles. "What will I do without you around to torture me?"

Nate slapped Quade's hand away and fixed his hair. "Suffer I guess."

Across the table, Ryan and Rio were challenging each other in a game of tonsil hockey. "I'll admit I'll miss not being in such an open environment."

Nate crossed his arms and cleared his throat until the two lovers broke apart. "Do you mind? We're trying to have a little going away party here."

"Sorry," Rio mumbled, wiping his mouth.

Quade leaned over and bumped shoulders with Nate, nearly knocking the small man out of the booth. "So, you gonna run for my position?"

"Mayor?" Nate asked with his hand to his chest.

"Of course you'd have to learn to deal with Carol," Quade added.

Nate chuckled. "I can handle Carol. I'm good with women."

Ryan choked on his beer as he and Rio roared with laughter.

Nate narrowed his eyes and reached across the table to run his finger up Ryan's forearm. "Would I have to challenge the sheriff on certain issues?"

"Occasionally," Quade said with a smile. "Does that interest you?"

"Mmmm, yes."

Ryan grunted and Nate giggled. Quade would vote for Nate in a heartbeat. He strongly suspected there were a lot of other people in town who would do the same. Oh to be a fly on the wall of those Sheriff's Department budget meetings. He'd definitely have to return to Cattle Valley, even if it was only once a year.

* * * *

"Oh my God. I can't believe you're finally here," Kai said, peppering kisses to Quade's face.

Quade gave Kai an enthusiastic kiss before stepping back. "Maybe we'd better save the rest of our hellos for someplace a little more private?"

Kai looked around at the other passengers standing beside the luggage carousel. "You're probably right," he agreed, taking Quade's hand. He couldn't believe Quade had managed to get enough time off work to fly with him to Australia at the end of the week.

"Are you tired?" Kai asked. Quade had missed his connecting flight in LA due to weather delays getting out of Wyoming. The resulting changes had added an extra four- hour layover in Los Angeles.

"Wiped, but not too much to give you a proper romp when we get home," Quade informed him, discreetly brushing their joined hands across the front of Kai's shorts.

"Oh good," Kai chuckled. "I'll admit I was a little worried."

Quade released Kai's hand when his suitcase came into view. *Man that's a huge piece of luggage,* Kai thought. He was further surprised when Quade hoisted another bag from the carousel.

Pushing his way through the crowd, Kai reached for one of the suitcases. "Man, did you bring me lots of presents or what?" Kai chuckled. Instead of trying to carry the bag, he pulled out the handle and rolled the suitcase back through the crowd of people.

"Something like that," Quade answered.

Presents? Kai loved gifts. He led the way to his jeep. After getting the over-sized bags stuffed into the back, he swung up behind the wheel. "Are you hungry? I can stop somewhere on the way home?"

Quade shook his head. "I bought a meal on the plane. I figured we wouldn't wanna take the time to eat."

"You figured right," Kai agreed, leaning over to steal a kiss. "Mmm," he moaned, thrusting his tongue deeper. He felt his cock harden painfully in his shorts. Breaking the kiss, he grinned. "If we don't leave now, I'll probably let you fuck me right here in the parking lot."

"Then drive, because another kiss like that and I probably will try to fuck you right here."

Feeling happier than he had in almost a month, Kai drove home. He kept his hands to himself until they carried the bags inside. Dropping the heavy suitcase on the floor, Kai began stripping his clothes off. "Naked. Now."

Kai was naked in no time and went to work on Quade's jeans, as his lover shucked his shirt and toed off his shoes. Easing the faded denim down Quade's hips, Kai was rewarded when the fat cock he loved so much sprang free.

Without waiting for an invitation, Kai's mouth immediately enveloped the head of Quade's erection. The taste of his lover's pre-cum burst with flavour on his tongue. "Mmm," he moaned, taking more of Quade's length into his mouth.

"Fuck," Quade grunted, fisting Kai's hair. "God I missed your mouth."

Kai smiled around the large cock and nodded. He reached out and clapped his hands on Quade's ass cheeks, pulling his lover closer, taking even more of him.

"It's been too long, babe. I won't last if you keep that up," Quade panted. He began a shallow thrust in and out of Kai's mouth.

The declaration only made Kai want it more. He pressed a finger against Quade's tightly puckered hole until the tip slipped inside.

"Aaahhh," Quade roared, coming down Kai's throat.

Kai continued to suck the softening cock until Quade pulled out. Kai was grabbed under the arms and lifted up into Quade's embrace. "That was one hell of a welcome."

"Oh, you ain't seen nothing yet. Wait 'til I get you into bed," Kai crooned, batting his lashes.

The luggage tossed onto the floor caught his attention. "So. Tell me what you brought me?"

Instead of opening the bags, Quade led Kai to the sofa. Kai settled himself on Quade's lap in his favourite position. "Well, aren't you gonna tell me?" he asked again.

Quade gave Kai a lopsided grin. "I can't believe it, but I'm suddenly nervous as hell."

Confused, Kai placed a kiss on the tip of Quade's nose. "Don't be nervous. I'm sure I'll love anything you brought."

"Yeah? What if I told you I brought you me?"

Kai reached down between them and cupped Quade's balls. "I think I've already proven how much I love this gift."

Quade gave a slight shake to his head. "That's not exactly what I meant."

"Oh? What then?"

"I quit my job. I thought I'd move to Oahu and become a surf groupie," he blurted.

Stunned, Kai sat back and gazed into Quade's eyes. "What? You love that job. Hell, you love that town."

"Yeah, but not nearly as much as I love the man in my arms. Going home to Charleston opened my eyes to a few things. Namely, that absolutely nothing in this life is more important than showing the people you love the attention they deserve."

Kai was so overcome with emotion he couldn't speak for several moments. Quade was right. "I can quit surfing. We can move back to Cattle Valley."

"No," Quade said, giving Kai a soft kiss. "I've done what I needed to do there, but your career is getting ready to take off. I'd like to make the journey with you if you'll have me?"

What an incredibly unselfish man he'd landed. "The journey wouldn't be nearly the same without you."

THE LAST
BOUQUET

Dedication

For my friends, Chel, Chris, Kelly and Deb.

Chapter One

With Puccini blaring in the background, Tyler Manning stared at the heart in his hands. Unlike most floral shops, Tyler had waited until the first week in February to decorate the front windows of his store for Valentine's Day.

The homemade decoration wasn't fancy, red velvet glued front and back to a big piece of cardboard. He'd found the most exquisite lace in Sheridan and had applied it around the perimeter of the four-foot heart.

Feeling the sudden urge to rip the heart down the middle, Tyler set it aside. Maybe decorating with a broken heart wasn't such a good idea. Visions of Hearn came to mind. Tyler gazed at the refrigerated case holding the weekly bouquet he made for Mitch's grave.

How had he managed to fall in love with a man who was already taken? "Fuck!" he yelled, kicking the heart at his feet.

Sinking to the floor, Tyler buried his face in his hands. Crying had become a regular habit lately. Since the accident that had killed Hearn's partner, Mitch, his friend had barely given him the time of day. If it weren't for the standing order of a bouquet of flowers, Tyler doubted he'd see Hearn at all. *Why?* It still didn't make sense to him.

Before the wreck, he and Hearn had become almost inseparable. Then Mitch had been killed and...nothing. At first Tyler worried that Hearn had picked up on his more than friendly feelings, but he no longer thought that was the case. It wasn't just Tyler that was being given the cold shoulder. Hearn had withdrawn so deep into himself and his charity work in Sheridan that no one ever saw him.

A hand on his shoulder startled Tyler, making him jump. "Easy," Hearn's smooth voice soothed.

Tyler gazed up into the same brown eyes he saw in his dreams every night. The concerned expression on Hearn's face as he knelt beside him melted Tyler right then and there.

"Are you okay?" Hearn asked over the loud music.

Feeling like an ass, Tyler nodded and wiped the tears from his face. "Yeah. Sorry." He stood and walked behind the counter to reduce the volume on La Boheme. Taking a deep breath, he turned to find Hearn standing right behind him.

"What's wrong?" Hearn asked.

Knowing he couldn't out and out lie to the man he loved, Tyler gestured around the shop. "Valentine's Day." He shrugged. "Depresses me every year."

The corner of Hearn's mouth rose slightly. "Kinda in the wrong business then aren't you?"

Unable to resist that sexy grin he enjoyed so much, Tyler smiled. "Yeah. I guess you're right."

Hearn put both hands on Tyler's shoulders and squeezed. "You'll find someone."

"I already have," Tyler admitted.

A look of dark emotions passed momentarily over Hearn's face before disappearing. "That's good, Ty, real good." Hearn released his hold on Tyler. "But if you're still feeling down enough to cry maybe this guy isn't the one for you."

"He is. He just doesn't know it yet." Tyler broke eye contact and walked towards the refrigerator. "Your flowers are ready," he announced, pulling out the large daisy and rose bouquet.

Hearn took the flowers, and just like he did every week, put them to his nose and inhaled. It was the moment Tyler both loved and hated every time. For that brief few seconds, all Hearn's problems seemed to melt into the background, leaving the gentle peaceful man Tyler had come to love.

"Bill me?" Hearn asked, opening his eyes.

"Of course," Tyler agreed. Trying to buy himself a few more moments in Hearn's company, Tyler scrambled for something to say. "Have you heard about Quade?"

Hearn stopped on his way to the door and turned. "No. Did something happen?"

"I'll say. He quit. It was announced earlier. I guess my cousin George is taking over for him until a special election is held."

Hearn whistled. "Wow. Why the hell didn't I see that one coming?"

"No one did. Quade decided to move to Oahu to be with that guy, Kai, he met last year." Tyler shifted from foot to foot. "I was thinking. Maybe this would be a good opportunity for you."

"Huh?"

"Well, you're always complaining the city doesn't have enough activities to keep the kids busy during the summer months. Maybe this is your chance to do something about it?"

"What. Like run for Mayor?" Hearn asked, dark brown eyes going wide.

"Yeah."

"I don't know the first thing about running a town." Hearn took several steps to stand on the opposite side of the counter from Tyler.

"You do so," Tyler disagreed. "You have a business degree. You run the entire park system like a well-oiled machine. You can do this," he implored, reaching out to grab Hearn's hand.

"I can't. Scheduling the sports fields and making sure the gazebos are cleaned isn't the same thing as running an entire town," Hearn said, shaking his head.

Tyler focused on the dark brown locks of hair as they fell back into place. Hearn had let his hair grow. He didn't know if it was by choice, or lack of caring, but Hearn's hair reached just past his shoulders to fall in a shaggy cascade.

"Tyler?"

"Yeah?"

"It makes me feel good to know you believe in me, but I'm honestly not qualified." Hearn pulled his hand out of Tyler's grip and held up the flowers. "I'll see you in a week."

Tyler watched Hearn walk out the door and pounded his fist against the counter. "Dammit!" Why couldn't Hearn see in himself what Tyler saw? The answer came to him with a bitter taste. "Mitch." The asshole who'd berated Hearn over and over for wasting his college education being a glorified groundskeeper. Why couldn't Hearn see that he'd been so much more than that to Cattle Valley?

Pushing away from the counter, Tyler turned the music back up and went back to work on his display. He'd figure out a way to undo all the years of damage living with Mitch had done to Hearn.

* * * *

Hearn stopped his pickup in the usual spot and gazed out over the small cemetery. He couldn't get the things Tyler had mentioned out of his mind. *Mayor?* Hearn shook off the fanciful thought and reached for the bundle of flowers at his side.

After zipping his coat, he opened the door and stepped onto the still-frozen ground. It was another cloudy dreary day, but it seemed to fit Hearn's mood perfectly. He'd spent the morning doing what he did every morning, driving to Sheridan to volunteer a couple of hours at the children's home.

Although he loved spending time with the kids, their sad eyes seemed to follow him home each day, especially that day. Gracie had managed to lose her one and only toy, a doll given to her by Hearn. The two of them had spent nearly two hours tracking down the little blonde-haired baby doll. Seeing the joy on Gracie's face had been worth the effort, but it had driven home the need to find the sweet girl a family of her own.

Before he knew it, Hearn stood at the foot of Mitch's grave. He bent over and picked up the dead arrangement and replaced it with the fresh one. What would the town think of him if they knew he brought flowers out of guilt, rather than love?

Walking away from the grave, Hearn tossed the dead bouquet into the trash on his way back to his truck. Forget the town. What would Tyler think of him if he knew the truth? Knowing the fight he'd had with Mitch that night had not only led to Mitch's death but put Tyler's life in danger as well, still shamed him.

Hearn shook his head, surprised to find himself in his truck with the engine running. His head was so full of Tyler Manning he barely had time to think of anything else. Seeing those brown puppy dog eyes crying earlier had almost sent him over the edge. All he'd wanted at that moment was to scoop Tyler from the floor and protect him against the world. The news that Tyler was interested in someone came as a shock. He didn't know why. Tyler was the sweetest man he'd ever known, the kind of man who deserved to find love. So why did it hurt so much? *Because I want to be that man.*

* * * *

Stepping into Brewster's, Tyler spotted a group of his friends and made his way across the room. "Mind if I join you?" he asked the group from the EZ Does It.

"Not at all," Wyn replied, gesturing to an empty chair.

Tyler smiled and sat down. "I haven't seen you and Ezra in here in months," he observed.

Wyn gestured towards the bar. "We like the new owner. He's been up to The Grizzly Bar a time or two, so we thought we'd return the favour."

"Well you won't be disappointed. Sean makes an excellent burger." He signalled to the waitress. "Can you grab me a cup of coffee when you get a chance?"

"Sure thing," Kitty said.

"So how're things going?" Wyn asked.

Tyler had liked Palmer Wynfield the first time he'd met him. The older man had taken him under his wing and introduced him to every store owner on Main Street. "Okay. I'm hoping business picks up for the fourteenth."

"It will," Wyn nodded. "But I was asking about you, not the shop."

"Oh." Tyler shrugged and peered down at his hands in his lap. Wyn was one of the few people who knew about his feelings for Hearn. "No change in that department. Hearn still takes flowers to Mitch's grave every week, and I'm still left out in the cold."

"I can't believe Hearn's still carrying a torch for that sonofabitch," Ezra scowled.

Tyler glanced up to see several people were staring at him. Evidently he'd spoken louder than he'd realised. The look of pity on the faces of his friends made him groan. "Am I that transparent?" he asked, unable to meet anyone's gaze.

Logan's tattooed forearm reached across the table and tilted Tyler's chin up. "There's nothing wrong with caring about someone."

"Yeah. Except when the one you care about is still in love with a dead man."

Jax surprised him by scooting his chair back and leaving the table. Tyler followed the man's back until he disappeared into the restroom. "Did I say something wrong?" he asked Logan.

"No. You might've just said something right." Logan stood. "If you'll excuse me."

Tyler watched Logan follow in Jax's footsteps. "Are they having problems?" he asked Wyn and Ezra.

"Not that I know of," Wyn replied.

Tyler was almost finished with his hamburger when he spotted an obviously upset Jax walking out of the restroom on Logan's arm. Instead of coming back to the table and their now-cold dinners, Logan led Jax out of the bar.

He noticed the expression on Ezra's face as his foreman left. Whatever was going on, Ezra knew about it. Tyler glanced to Wyn, who still appeared oblivious to his partner's worried stare. Ezra caught Tyler's gaze and held it. "I think we need to talk."

* * * *

With his car idling in the cold winter's night, Tyler waited for Jax and Logan to immerge from Hearn's house. He knew if he had bigger balls, he'd walk right up to the front door and knock with the two visitors still inside, but he was a chicken.

Hell, he'd always shied away from confrontation. It was probably the reason he'd allowed himself to be used by so many men in the past. *Face it, Manning, you're a pussy.* As a kid he'd been beat up by practically everyone in his class at one time or another, both boys and girls. His father had tried on several occasions to teach him how to defend himself, but Tyler never could bring himself to fight back.

It wasn't that he was afraid of getting hit. It was the anger he couldn't stand. Whenever someone started yelling, Tyler's gut immediately began to cramp. On more than one occasion, he'd actually thrown up before the first punch knocked him to the ground.

So here he sat, all five-foot-five-inches of himself, waiting for Jax and Logan to leave. He didn't know what he'd say to Hearn once the two men were gone, but he knew in his heart he needed to be here for his friend.

A lump formed in his throat as he watched the front door open and the two men get into their truck. Staring at the silhouetted forms embracing, Tyler felt like an intruder. He knew it hadn't been easy for Jax to come clean with Hearn about his affair with Mitch, but just then, Tyler didn't give a fuck about Jax. He just needed the men to leave so he could check on Hearn.

Finally, after another ten minutes, Logan pulled the truck out of Hearn's driveway. Tyler waited until the taillights rounded the corner before getting out of his five-year old Civic.

By the time he crossed the street and walked up the porch steps, Tyler's stomach was in knots. Maybe this wasn't a good idea? What if Hearn didn't need him?

Pushing his fears away, Tyler took a deep breath and knocked on the door. When Hearn didn't answer, Tyler leaned over and watched through the living room window. Hearn sat on the couch, his hands balled into fists, staring straight ahead.

"Hearn?" he finally called out, knocking on the glass.

The much bigger man blinked several times before meeting Tyler's gaze through the window. "Can I come in?"

Hearn gazed at him for several moments before standing. Tyler straightened and stood in front of the door. Hearn's facial expression when he opened the door scared Tyler. He felt the bile rise from his stomach to his throat.

"What do you want, Ty?" Hearn asked, his voice barely above a whisper.

"Can I come in?"

Hearn stepped back and Tyler squeezed past him and into the living room. He didn't know how to break the news to Hearn that he knew what Mitch had done. "I...I was at Brewster's when Jax and Logan left."

Tyler tugged off his stocking cap and jammed it into his coat pocket. "Ezra told me about Mitch."

"He had no right!" Hearn exploded.

With a hand held against his queasy stomach, Tyler nodded. "Ezra was worried about you. He thought you might need a friend."

Hearn's gaze met Tyler's for the first time since he'd opened the door. "Are they laughing at me?"

"No!" Tyler exclaimed, rushing to Hearn's side. "I told you, they're worried. News that the man you loved wasn't faithful…it would devastate anyone."

Hearn started to chuckle, confusing Tyler. When the chuckle turned into a full-blown belly laugh, Tyler started to get scared for the sanity of the man he loved.

"I haven't been in love with Mitch for years," Hearn confessed, knocking a vase off the nearby table.

The action made Tyler jump. The obvious rage inside Hearn was more than Tyler's stomach could handle. Cupping a hand over his mouth, Tyler sprinted towards the bathroom. He barely got the toilet seat up before he lost his entire dinner in the bowl.

Resting his head on the cold porcelain, Tyler tried to calm himself. He knew Hearn wasn't mad at him, it was Mitch Hearn hated at the moment.

A large hand landed on his back. "Are you okay?" Hearn asked, all traces of anger gone.

God, he felt like an ass. Here he'd come over to comfort Hearn and he was the one being comforted. "I'm okay," Tyler lied, flushing the stool. "I've never handled anger well. Stupid, I know."

From their position on the floor, Hearn reached up and wet a washcloth. After wringing it out with one hand, he began cleaning Tyler's face. "Nothing stupid about that. I let myself lose control, and I'm sorry you suffered for it."

"You've earned the right to lose control."

Hearn tossed the washcloth to the side and reached for a bottle of mouthwash, passing it to Tyler. "You're right. I have earned the right to be angry with Mitch, but that doesn't mean I should take it out on you."

Tyler took a big swig of the minty mouthwash before spitting it into the toilet. "Don't apologise for that. I came over because I thought you might need a friend."

"Can you stand?" Hearn asked, getting to his feet.

"Yeah." With Hearn's help, Tyler stood. In the small space provided, Tyler was practically sandwiched against Hearn's tall frame. He hadn't stood this close to the man since the night of Kyle and Gill's wedding reception, when Hearn had danced with him.

Without thinking, Tyler rested his cheek against Hearn's broad chest. "Thank you," he whispered, wrapping his arms around Hearn's waist.

Hearn returned the embrace, resting his own cheek on top of Tyler's head. "No. Thank you. Knowing what I now know, it was pretty brave of you to come over here to check on me."

"You're the most important person in the world to me. Of course I came," Tyler admitted.

He felt Hearn's entire body tense. "What did you say?"

Shit! The last thing Hearn needed was a declaration of love at a time like this. "I said you're important to me. You may not know it, but you're my best friend."

Hearn kissed the top of Tyler's head. "You're my best friend, too."

Chapter Two

Nate was putting the finishing touches on dinner when Ryan came through the door. "Mmm. Something smells good."

Nate spun around and lifted his chin. "It's the new cologne I picked up at Wyn's."

Chuckling, Ryan buried his face in Nate's neck. "Yep, that smells pretty damn good, but I was talking about dinner."

"So was I," Nate quipped, cupping Ryan's cock through his jeans.

Ryan's mouth latched onto the skin just below Nate's ear. While his lover busied himself sucking up a bruise, Nate took the opportunity to unzip Ryan's jeans.

Ryan pulled his mouth from Nate's neck and moaned. "Feels good, baby."

"Damn right it does," Nate agreed, pumping the shaft in his hand. Sinking to his knees, Nate pushed Ryan's jeans down until his lover's erection sprang free. "Mmm. Yummy," he giggled, running his tongue from root to crown. After enjoying the taste of Ryan's pre-cum, Nate's lips slipped over the tip.

A cold breeze stirred the air moments before another cock jabbed his cheek. Nate opened his eyes and looked up to see Rio thrusting his tongue down Ryan's throat. Grinning around the girth in his mouth, he wrapped his fingers around the bouncing cock in front of him.

The cold feel of Rio's length surprised him. Releasing Ryan's cock, he blew hot air on Rio's erection. "Poor baby's almost frozen."

"It's fucking cold outside," Rio defended.

"I know it is," Nate placated. "Thank you for feeding the horses." He leaned in and swallowed Rio's length. He was really getting into it when a finger began tapping the top of his head. "What?" he asked, abandoning his work.

"As hot as that little mouth of yours is, the dinner is hotter." Rio gestured towards the smoking oven.

"Shit!" Nate cried, jumping to his feet. He narrowed his eyes at Ryan as he grabbed a pot holder and pulled his burnt chicken out of the oven. Dropping the roasting pan onto the counter, he propped his hands on his hips. "Well, that sucks."

Ryan wrapped his arms around Nate's waist. "It doesn't look too bad. We'll just scrape off the black stuff."

Nate shrugged. "I guess so."

"Why don't you help Rio set the table, and I'll take care of the chicken," Ryan offered, kissing Nate's neck.

He knew he was a bit of a perfectionist, but he loved giving his men a meal fit for kings at the end of their day. Nate nodded and reached for the dishes. After handing the stack to Rio, he turned to face Ryan. "Do you want me to help you with the side dishes?"

Ryan shook his head. "I'll take care of it, baby. You just suck that pretty little bottom lip back in and let Rio take care of you."

Nate grinned. "Can I make him do anything I want?"

Ryan glanced over at Rio who was setting the plates on the table. "Do you even have to ask?"

Nate clapped his hands. "Well then, I'm off to put my pout on."

Ryan rolled his eyes and gave Nate a swat on the ass as he walked away. Rubbing his butt, Nate stuck his bottom lip out even further and got out the silverware. Strolling towards the table, he began placing the eating utensils on either side of the plates.

Rio pulled out one of the dining room chairs and sat down. "Come over here, little man," Rio said, patting his lap.

Nate was giggling his ass off on the inside, but he didn't dare let his glee show on the outside. It had taken him a long time to learn each man's weak spots, but he'd become an expert at exploiting them for his own sexual gain.

Settling himself in Rio's lap, Nate tilted his chin up for a kiss. Rio wasted no time delving his tongue deep into Nate's mouth. Pulling back, Rio grinned. "Just for the record. I know you're playing me like a violin right now, but you're so damn cute I don't mind."

Nate winced. "The lip too much?"

"Just a tad. Besides, it's not all our fault you were greedily munching on our cocks instead of watching your dinner."

Nate crossed his arms. "Don't hold your breath until the next time I decide to *munch* your cock."

"Like you could stay away," Rio chuckled.

He's got me. Nate threw his arms around Rio's neck and kissed him. "You're right. I'd starve without my daily dose of protein."

"Oh, God," Ryan drawled as he set the platter of chicken on the table. "Get off Papa Bear's lap, Goldislut, and eat your porridge."

Laughing, Rio pinched Nate's ass. "You heard Mama Bear, get up."

Giggling, Nate jumped up and moved to his chair. "Aww, this fits just right," he joked. Although the dinner he'd prepared wasn't perfect, Nate couldn't wait another minute to talk to his men. "Sooo, I was thinking today..."

"Oh no. How much is it gonna cost us?" Ryan interrupted.

"Would you let me finish." He slapped him on the arm. "I want to run for mayor," he stated before bracing himself for the teasing that was sure to come.

Rio and Ryan looked at each other. They seemed to be having some sort of Vulcan mind meld right before his eyes. Finally, Ryan reached out and took Nate's hand. "You'd be a fantastic mayor."

"Really? You think so?" He'd never been so happy to have been wrong in his life. The fact Rio and Ryan supported his decision meant everything to him. "I mean. I know I don't have a lot of experience, but I think I could make a real difference."

"You could. And don't sell yourself short. You're good with people, you have a head for business and you may be the one person in all of Cattle Valley who could endear himself to Carol." Ryan grinned and took a bite of his rosemary potatoes.

* * * *

Hearn handed Tyler a cup of coffee. "I put a little Bailey's in it. I know you like it, and I thought we could both use something to take the edge off."

"Thanks."

The way Tyler was curled up with his feet tucked up under him, made the man appear even smaller. Hearn had never thought of himself as oversized, but compared to Tyler, he felt like a giant. He remembered the first time he'd ever laid eyes on the florist. It was before the floral shop even opened its doors. He'd just picked up another Christmas present for Mitch from Wynfield's Department Store, when he spotted a wood nymph among a sea of realistic evergreen trees. Curious, he'd crossed the street and peered at the small man in the window of the old flower shop. Tyler had smiled and waved, dropping one of the artificial trees on his foot. He'd gestured for Hearn to come in. Stepping into that store had forever changed his life.

"Hearn? Are you okay?" Tyler asked from his position on the sofa.

"Yeah." Hearn sat next to Tyler and took a sip of his cooling coffee. "I was just remembering the day we met."

Tyler's entire face lit up from within. "I remember that. I was a klutz and dropped one of the display pieces onto my foot."

"A tree. It was one of those artificial trees you put in the window," Hearn added.

Tyler smiled and nodded in remembrance. "I wasn't near ready to open the shop, but I didn't want the windows empty at Christmas time."

The smaller man gazed down into his coffee. "I was working away, and I happened to look up into the deepest brown eyes I'd ever seen." Tyler chuckled. "Anyone would've forgotten what they were doing with a view like that."

Hearn didn't know how to reply to such a statement. He'd never thought of himself as overly gorgeous. He knew he had a few good features, but the overall package had never seemed like something to brag about. Maybe if it had Mitch wouldn't have gone looking. "Why do you think he did it?"

With a deep breath, Tyler set his cup on the table. "Mitch?"

"Yeah."

Tyler reached out and held Hearn's hand. Damn Tyler's skin was soft, his fingers so thin and long.

"It wasn't you," Tyler offered.

Hearn opened his mouth to argue, but Tyler cut him off. "Cheating isn't about the person being cheated on. It's about the person doing the cheating. Evidently, Mitch didn't feel good about himself. He needed to find as many people as possible to reaffirm his self-worth."

As many people as possible? "Wait," he said, shaking his head. "Jax wasn't the only one?"

Tyler's eyes rounded. "I'm sorry. I thought Jax told you."

Hearn didn't know how it was possible, but his chest constricted even more than it had earlier. He'd been able to pass Mitch's infidelity off as falling in love with another man. After all, wasn't he just as guilty of that crime, but to hear there were others... "How many?"

Tyler shrugged. "I don't know. Ezra just told me Jax wasn't the only one Mitch had secret rendezvous' with."

How many, Mitch? Did you at least wear a fucking condom? Why didn't I see it? The answer was sitting right in front of him. *Because I was too busy falling in love with my new best friend.*

He gazed into Tyler's chocolate brown eyes. Hearn had always been fascinated by the man's lashes, and the way they fanned over his cheeks every time he blinked. No. He couldn't blame anything on Tyler. According to Jax, the affair between him and Mitch had gone on for years. Tyler had only been in town for a little over a year.

Hearn thought about the late nights Mitch often kept. His partner had always had a plausible excuse, a dinner meeting that ran long, car trouble, or the weather, it was always something. Hearn had never dwelt on it because the truth was, he enjoyed the evenings Mitch wasn't home. His lover was constantly bitching at him for something. Some shortfall he felt Hearn needed to change. How many evenings had he secretly wished for something that would give him the strength to leave?

155

"I wish I'd known. My life with Mitch sucked the last several years we were together, but we'd been partners since college. I tried to ride out the rough patches. I felt I owed him that." He laughed. "Evidently Mitch had a different kind of riding in mind."

Tyler squeezed his hand. "You're a better man than he was."

Sobering, Hearn returned the squeeze. Tyler had been a loyal friend since they'd met. Even after the accident when Hearn had tried his best to push the smaller man away, Tyler never stopped trying. "He meant to do it you know."

Tyler's head tilted to the side in question. "Do what?"

"Run into that tree," Hearn confessed. He'd carried the secret too long. If he did nothing else right in his life, he knew he needed to tell Tyler the truth about that night.

Tyler's entire body seemed to tense up. "I know," Tyler whispered.

"You do?"

Tyler nodded. "He confronted me before we got into the car."

Now it was Hearn's turn to tense. "About the talk he and I had after I danced with you?" Had Tyler really known of his feelings all this time?

Tyler appeared more confused than ever. "I didn't know the two of you had talked."

"What exactly did he say to you?" Hearn asked.

Tyler broke eye contact and studied the flames flickering in the fireplace. "I was trying to find you in the crowd. Mitch found me first. He grabbed my arm and told me he knew."

Hearn swallowed around the lump in his throat. "Knew what?"

"That I'd fallen in love with you. He told me I couldn't have you. That he'd worked too long to gain your trust." Tyler stopped and shook his head. "Actually, what he said was that he'd worked too long to gain your trust fund, but I thought he'd just made a mistake."

My trust fund? While trying to let that bit of information sink in, he realised he'd bypassed the most important part of Tyler's statement. "Are you?"

"Am I what," Tyler mumbled, still refusing to look at Hearn.

Hearn cupped Tyler's cheek and turned the smaller man's attention back to him. "Are you in love with me?"

Tyler's jaw dropped before snapping shut. When it appeared Tyler wasn't going to answer, Hearn continued. "Because the night of the accident, I told Mitch I was planning to move out." Hearn slid his hand to the back of Tyler's neck and pulled him closer. "I confessed that I'd fallen in love with my best friend."

The truth of Hearn's words seemed to dawn in Tyler's eyes moments before Hearn kissed him. He didn't push things, choosing to keep the kiss short and sweet.

When he pulled back, Tyler's eyes were filled with tears. "Why didn't you tell me before?" Tyler asked.

"It was because of what I'd told him that Mitch purposely ran into that tree. I didn't know he'd been fucking around on the side. I thought I'd betrayed him. That the thought of losing me had driven him to do it."

A single tear slid down Tyler's cheek. Hearn swiped the moisture away with his thumb. "Now I'm not sure why he did it. Maybe his goal was to kill one of us, maybe it was to injure himself enough that I wouldn't leave." Hearn shrugged. "We may never know."

"It killed me to watch you mourn for that man as long as you did. He treated you like shit when he was alive. Never giving you enough credit for the intelligent man I know you are."

Hearn gave Tyler's hand a tug until the smaller man was seated on his lap. "You will know the truth, and the truth will set you free," he quoted.

Tyler grinned and buried his face against Hearn's neck. "I never thought I'd get the chance to be here, like this."

Despite Tyler's words, Hearn remembered what they'd talked about earlier in the day. "So, who's this new guy you have your eye on?" He wondered if it was someone Tyler had met in the months following Mitch's death.

"Not a new guy," Tyler mumbled. "It's you. It's always been you."

Hearn could almost feel his fractured heart begin to mend. "As much as I'd like to take you into the bedroom and ask you to prove it, I won't. I'd like to ask you out on a proper date first."

"A date?" Tyler asked.

Hearn could feel Tyler smile against his neck moments before soft kisses landed on his heated skin. Hearn's hold on the smaller man tightened. The image of his little wood nymph under him was almost more than he could bear and still maintain control. Tyler deserved more than a hasty fuck. He'd proven worthy of a proper courting first.

When Tyler's kisses became licks, Hearn groaned. "I'm trying to be a gentleman, but you're not making it easy."

"Chivalry is overrated," Tyler answered back. "I've dreamed of this moment for too long to let it slip through my fingers without at least getting a taste of you."

Tyler's hands began working their way under Hearn's T-shirt. If Hearn's cock weren't already painfully hard, the gentle pinch to his nipples would've done the trick. His hands went to Tyler's hips, pushing the little sprite down against the bulging fly of his jeans. The press of that sweet little ass against his throbbing erection, snapped every ounce of his reserve.

Grabbing the bottom of Tyler's long-sleeved sport shirt, Hearn pulled the soft cotton over his soon-to-be lover's head. Just as he'd hoped, Tyler's chest was sleek and hair-free. "Oh, shit," Hearn panted, running his fingers over the smooth skin.

"Sorry," Tyler mumbled. "I've never been accused of having a manly physique."

"You're perfect." Hearn's touch travelled across Tyler's dark brown nipples, to the thin line of hair trailing down below his belly button. He wanted, no, needed, to see more. "May I?" he asked, hands poised on the button of Tyler's jeans.

Tyler licked his lips and grinned. "What? No steak first?" he asked with a chuckle.

Hearn immediately pulled his hands back. "I'm sorry. I guess I just got carried away."

Laughing, Tyler reached down and unfastened his own jeans. "I was kidding."

"Maybe so, but I can't do what I'd like to anyway, no condoms. With everything I've learned about Mitch..." Hearn shook his head. "Guess I need to be tested."

"I get tested every six months whether I'm active or not. The last one was before Thanksgiving. I'm clean," Tyler declared.

Hearn gave a short nod. "Well then we just need to wait for my results. Until then, maybe it would be better if we stuck to necking like a couple of teenagers."

Tyler rolled his eyes. "Kissing's always felt better than fucking anyway."

Surprised, Hearn pulled Tyler in for a kiss, sweeping his tongue through the interior of the smaller man's mouth. Groaning, Tyler began sucking on Hearn's tongue. Hearn answered by opening even wider. The pressure from Tyler's teeth against his stretched mouth split his lip. The metallic taste of blood snapped Hearn out of his lust-haze. Breaking the kiss, he immediately ran his tongue around his lips until he found the small slit in the skin. "Maybe kissing before my results are back isn't such a good idea either."

"Maybe not."

Trying to resist the lure of those pretty pink lips, Hearn hugged Tyler to his chest. "By the way, if kissing feels better to you than fucking, someone should be ashamed of themselves."

"Hmmm, maybe I've just been waiting for you?" Tyler replied around a yawn.

Hearn kissed Tyler's forehead. "Maybe." He gave Tyler a playful squeeze on the ass. "You'd better go home and get some rest."

"I don't want the night to end," Tyler mumbled.

"Neither do I, but I'm trying my damndest to put your safety above my own needs. I have a feeling if you stay much longer, my good intentions will be lost."

Tyler slid off Hearn's lap and refastened his jeans. "Call me when you wake up?"

"I'll do one better. I'll stop in and take ya to lunch, maybe get a little kissing in before we eat."

Tyler lifted his shirt from the couch and pulled it over his head. Sitting on the sofa to put his athletic shoes on, he bumped Hearn with his shoulder. "Can you do me a favour and ask Isaac to put a rush on that test?"

"Definitely."

Chapter Three

"Hello? Anyone here?" Nate called out, standing in the middle of the empty reception area.

George Manning opened the door to Quade's old office. "Hey, Nate. Carol just left to grab us a couple sandwiches from Deb's. Is there something I can help you with?"

"Uh, yeah, I wanted to ask if she had the paperwork I need to fill out to get on the mayoral ballot?"

George's black brows rose. "Really? You thinking about running?"

"Yeah." Nate shrugged. "I talked it over with Rio and Ryan and they told me to go for it."

"Great," George said, going to the shelf beside Carol's desk. "You'd be a good choice for the position." He handed Nate a small stack of papers. "You'll need to fill these out and pay the running fee. It's not much so you shouldn't have any problems. When you're done, just bring 'em back here and Carol will make it official."

"Thanks."

"No problem," George replied with a wave as Nate turned to leave.

Nate climbed into his SUV, laid the forms on the passenger seat and drove to The Gym. Parking in his usual spot, he noticed the place appeared pretty dead. It wasn't unusual for that time of day. He knew the place would be packed within an hour as businessmen and women came in on their lunch hours, all hoping to shed the pounds they'd picked up over the holidays.

He spotted Mario and Rio sitting at the juice counter, playing a friendly game of cards. "Don't the two of you have anything better to do?" he asked, pressing himself against Rio's heavily muscled back.

"Nope," Rio said, laying down a fan of cards. "Gin."

"Shit," Mario spat and threw his cards on the counter.

Chuckling, Rio took the pencil from behind his ear and scratched his score on a pad of paper.

"So what's the damage?" Mario asked.

"Two private kick-boxing classes and one spin class," Rio informed him, turning the pad around so Mario could see for himself.

"Shit." Mario stood and gathered the cards. "Remind me to do sit-ups next time I get bored."

"Hey, if you're nice and don't pout I'll let you have your choice of which lessons to take over for me."

Mario grinned, flashing those perfectly white teeth. "I can choose, really?"

Chuckling, Rio nodded. "Yep. Asa comes on Tuesdays and Thursdays at six. If you impress him, maybe he'll ask for you from now on."

Mario rubbed his hands together. "I'll have to bone-up on my skills."

Nate burst out laughing. "Believe me, if you're working with Asa you'll already be boned up. You've had a thing for that man since the first day he came in here."

Mario's face turned a delightful shade of red. "That noticeable, huh?"

Nate walked over and gave Mario a hug. "Only to the people who love you."

Giving him a hug back, Mario kissed Nate's cheek. "Thanks. You guys are like family to me, too."

After Mario left to get ready for the onslaught of the New Year's resolutioners, he turned back to Rio. "I stopped by City Hall and picked up the papers."

"That's good," Rio said, holding out his arms.

Nate gleefully accepted the invitation. Life always felt better in the comfort of Rio's embrace. The butterflies in his stomach from earlier still hadn't calmed. "I can't believe how nervous I am. I'm never nervous."

Running soothing hands up and down Nate's spine, Rio kissed him. "Makes sense you'd be a little worried. It's an important position."

Nate shook his head. "It's not that. It just reminds me too much of high school. Did I ever tell you I ran for class president?"

"Ran? Does that mean you didn't win?" Rio asked.

"Right. I was creamed in the voting by a jock named Steve Hurley. Hell, the guy didn't even know what a class president did, but they elected him anyway."

Rio began nibbling on Nate's ear. "What kind of fools did you go to school with?"

"Homophobic assholes."

Rio pulled back, an expression of surprise on his face. "You were *out* in high school?"

God, I should've never brought it up. He'd never talked about his past with his partners other than to say he no longer had contact with his parents. He knew Rio and Ryan figured it was due to him being gay, but Nate knew that was only the tip of the iceberg. He'd suffered enough looks of disgust and pity over the years, the last thing he wanted was to see it in his lovers' eyes.

"Yeah," he finally mumbled. "I wouldn't recommend it."

"What, no date for the prom?" Rio chuckled.

Nate tried to control his reaction to the question. If his lover knew how much it hurt, the big soft-hearted man would feel terrible. "I didn't go to the prom."

Rio, bless his heart, still hadn't caught on to the fact it was a sore subject. "I'm surprised that in a city the size of Chicago there wasn't at least one other gay guy in your school to go with."

Nate broke away from Rio's embrace and walked behind the counter. Turning his back to his partner, he dug in the fridge for a bottle of water. He couldn't get the picture of Joseph out of his head. The last time he'd seen his first lover was from across a conference table. They'd made them both sign papers that they would never see each other again. Nate wasn't the only one who'd wept that day. Joseph's bright blue eyes had been clouded with pain and longing. The image of the normally cheerful man, sad and broken, would forever haunt Nate.

"Can we talk about something else?" he asked, rubbing the cold bottle against his forehead.

Strong arms encircled his waist. "Are you okay?" Rio asked.

Nate nodded. "Just a sore subject that I'd rather not discuss." He didn't tell Rio he'd signed legal documents preventing him. He wasn't a child anymore. Nate knew the papers weren't preventing him from disclosing the details to his partners. He simply didn't talk about it out of self-preservation.

Rio's arms tightened. *Damn.* He knew his gentle giant felt guilty. Nope. That would never do. Nate knew he was the *fun* in the relationship. If he allowed himself to slip back into the depression that had plagued him for years, he wouldn't be anything special, just a geeky guy with a fabulous taste in clothes.

Putting his *fun* face on, Nate spun in Rio's arms. "Do we have time for a quickie before the hordes arrive?"

* * * *

Dressed in a yellow paper gown, Hearn patiently waited for Dr. Singer. He still didn't understand why Isaac insisted on giving him an exam. All he'd wanted was a damn blood test, not a physical.

The door opened and the handsome older man stepped into the room. "Good to see you," Isaac greeted, shaking Hearn's hand.

"You, too." Hearn shifted on the exam table, feeling the cold white paper covering the table crinkle under his bare ass. "I have to say I was surprised I needed a physical just to get a blood test."

Isaac sat on the short black stool and linked his fingers. "Normally you don't, but you've been through a hell of a year. I just needed to know you've been taking care of yourself."

"I feel fine," Hearn answered. He thought of Tyler and smiled. "Actually, I'm happier than I have been in years."

Isaac grinned. "Yeah? And does this new-found happiness have anything to do with wanting an HIV test?"

"Maybe."

Isaac's brows rose, but the distinguished doctor said nothing more, obviously waiting for Hearn to spill the beans. With a resigned sigh, Hearn spilled. "I'm finally planning to act on my feelings for Tyler Manning."

Chuckling, Isaac reached out and slapped Hearn's knee. "It's about damn time. And you couldn't have picked a better guy. I worked a lot with him on the AIDS walk we organised last fall. He's incredibly giving, always looking out for the best interest of the community. Tyler's everything a parent could hope for in a son."

"I'm a lucky man," Hearn agreed. He noticed the time on Isaac's watch. "Actually, can we move this along so I can make my lunch date with the man of my dreams?" he asked, smiling.

"Sure. Let's not have it said that I stood in the way of true love," Isaac joked, taking out his stethoscope.

Thirty minutes later, Hearn walked out of the clinic and down the street to the floral shop. One thing continued to stand out from his conversation with Isaac. Tyler was a very civic-minded individual.

Hearn had always known that, but hearing it from someone else only proved to drive the point home.

He'd spent years listening to Mitch degrade him for his lack of drive and intelligence. He loved running the park system in Cattle Valley, but it had never seemed to matter to Mitch. Hearn wondered if it mattered to Tyler. Was it the reason Tyler wanted him to run for mayor?

Before he knew it, he stood in front of the display window. "Wow." Tyler had obviously been busy. The window had been transformed into a sea of red hearts and fresh flowers.

The brass bell signalled his arrival as he stepped into the shop. His gaze immediately zeroed in on the man behind the counter. The red cashmere sweater showed off Tyler's smaller size to perfection.

Tyler paused in his conversation with a customer to acknowledge him. "Give me a few minutes?"

"Sure. I'll just look around," he answered. Hearn wandered over to the display of stuffed animals. Picking up a fluffy little lamb, he thought of Gracie and smiled. He felt bad for not visiting the young girl that morning, but maybe a gift would make it up to her.

Idly rubbing the animal's soft wool against his chin, Hearn continued to browse the gifts and other home accents on display.

"Soft isn't it?" Tyler noted, stepping up behind Hearn.

Hearn realised what he'd been doing and pulled the lamb away from his face. "Yeah. There's a little girl I'm quite taken with that would love it."

"Oh really? You holding out on me?" Tyler teased.

Hearn glanced around the shop before wrapping his arms around Tyler. "I've been spending a lot of time at the Sheridan Home for Children lately. There's an angel who lives there who's stolen my heart."

Tyler grinned. "Should I be jealous?"

Tilting his head, Hearn peered out the window. "Ummm, no. But I guarantee Gracie would steal your heart, too. I think she must be a collector. She has the entire staff wrapped around her little six-year-old finger."

"Would it be callous of me to ask why she's there?" Tyler asked.

"Social Services removed her from her mother's custody. I guess when she first arrived at the centre she was in pretty bad shape. She'd been abused, both mentally and physically. Even though she was four at the time, she was the size of a two and a half year old."

"Why haven't they placed her in a foster home?" Tyler asked, tears in his eyes.

"They tried. Several times actually, but Gracie doesn't trust many people. She seems to have a real problem with women, but who can blame her." Hearn shrugged. "So I go almost every day and give her all the attention I can. She's slowly coming out of her shell, but she has a long way to go."

Tyler stood on his tip-toes and pulled Hearn's head down for a kiss. The sweep of his lover's tongue ignited Hearn's passion. How many times had he come into the shop and longed to kiss the man he'd fallen so hard for? With his hands on Tyler's ass, Hearn lifted the smaller man for a deeper kiss.

Breaking for air, Tyler grinned. "Unless you plan on spending the rest of the day upstairs at my place, I think we'd better go eat."

Hearn reluctantly set Tyler back onto his feet. "Guess we'd better." He pressed another kiss to Tyler's lips. "But I'll be back when you close up."

Tyler bent and picked up the stuffed animal. "I'll get my coat and put this into a bag for you."

Hearn started to get out his wallet, but Tyler stopped him. "No. Let me do this."

"You don't have to," Hearn informed Tyler.

"Of course I don't," Tyler replied, slipping the lamb into a lavender bag. "I want to." Tyler handed the sack to Hearn. "I'll just get my coat."

Once more, Hearn was reminded how good a man he'd fallen for. Tyler never seemed to think of himself first. *I want to be that kind of man.*

"Ready?" Tyler asked, dressed in his winter coat.

"Yep." Hearn led the way out to the sidewalk and waited for Tyler to lock the store. Taking the smaller man's hand, they walked next door to Deb's.

After getting seated, Hearn took a sip of his water. He still couldn't believe he was actually considering this. "I've been thinking about what you mentioned earlier. You know, about me running for mayor. Even though my business skills are a bit rusty, I think I'll do it."

With excitement written all over his face, Tyler clapped his hands together. "Really? I thought you'd decided against it."

Hearn picked up the salt shaker and poured a dab on the napkin under his drink. You couldn't have a serious discussion with a napkin stuck to the sweaty glass you were drinking from. "I know what I said. And I'm still not convinced I'm the best man for the job, but you were right. It's time to put up or shut up. It's really the only way I can guarantee my park proposals will get before the council. I'd miss running the parks, but I'd be in a much better position to improve them."

Tyler reached across the table and squeezed Hearn's hand. "I'm so proud of you."

Gazing into Tyler's eyes, Hearn knew that was the reason he was running in the first place. What would it be like to have a lover proud of him for the first time in his life?

"I'll go by City Hall after I drop you back by the store."

Tyler ran a foot up the inside of Hearn's calf. "Maybe you could run by Asher's Pharmacy after that and pick up a few things."

Grinning, Hearn winked. "Why, Mr. Manning, are you planning to seduce me later?"

"That's exactly what I'm planning. I thought I'd make you a nice home cooked dinner at my place." Tyler stood and leaned over the table to give Hearn a quick kiss. "Pack your vitamins and an overnight bag."

* * * *

Sitting on the floor of his closet, Nate glanced at the birth certificate in his hands. Maybe he should rethink this whole thing? When he'd told his partners he wanted to run for mayor, he had no idea he'd have to produce a copy of his birth certificate.

He'd even called Carol to try and get out of attaching it to the application. He'd argued that a passport should be good enough, but Carol told him they had to follow the guidelines which specifically called for a certified copy of the applicant's birth record.

William Nathaniel Gilloume. How long had it been since someone called him by his real name? He knew the answer immediately. The day he'd graduated from high school, the same day his father had given him a sizeable check, laying out the conditions of accepting the money.

Setting the certificate aside, Nate reached back into the box for the photo he knew was safely tucked in an envelope. It had been a couple of years since he'd last pulled the old picture out of its hiding place.

The tears that ran down his face were normal. Looking at Joseph's picture always brought back too many memories. "I miss you," he whispered to the photograph. How old had his first lover been when this picture was taken, twenty-four, twenty-five?

"Are you in here?" Ryan called out from the bedroom.

I have to tell them the truth. "I'm in here." Nate put the photo back into its envelope and picked up the box. "I'll be out in a second."

Before he could get his emotions under control, Ryan appeared beside him. "What're you doing, baby?"

"Taking a stroll down Memory Lane," he answered. "Is Rio home yet?" He knew he needed to confess his sins before chickening out.

"Yeah. We noticed you hadn't started dinner, so he's whipping up his famous tuna casserole." Ryan turned Nate to face him. "What's going on?"

"If I run for mayor, it might come out who I really am."

Chapter Four

Hearn was surprised to find the door that opened onto the street unlocked. With a shake of his head, he started up the steep staircase towards Tyler's apartment over the floral shop.

In all the time he'd known Tyler, it was hard to believe he'd never been to his place. He was happy to see another door at the top of the steps. He needed to talk to Tyler about keeping the street-level door locked. Even though crime in Cattle Valley was almost non-existent, it never hurt to be cautious.

Switching his overnight bag to his other hand, he knocked on the solid wood door. Before his hand had time to reach his side, the door opened with a whoosh.

"Right on time," Tyler greeted him.

The smell of pizza in the room was a bit of a surprise though. "Pizza? I thought you were making me a home cooked meal?"

Tyler pulled him into the room and kissed him. "I was going to, but I decided to leave that for our second date."

Hearn grinned. "You're just in a hurry to get into my pants."

"That's exactly right," Tyler agreed. The smaller man gestured towards the living room of the loft-style apartment. "Make yourself at home, and I'll get us something to drink. Pizza's on the coffee table so help yourself."

Looking around, Hearn was impressed. The loft was small, but Tyler had done a damn good job making the most of it. "Did you do all this by yourself?" he asked, taking off his coat.

Shutting the refrigerator, Tyler's gaze roamed the room. "I had some help, but yeah."

Hearn glanced at the raised platform in the corner of the room. "Nice bed," he commented, sitting on the cream-colored sectional. He opened the large box on the table and withdrew a slice of pizza. He could hear Tyler moving around behind him so he figured he was expected to just start eating.

A nude Tyler bounded over the back of the sofa and handed Hearn a bottle of beer. "Glad you like it. I thought I'd serve dessert there."

With a big bite of pizza in his mouth, Hearn nearly choked. He'd never known this side of Tyler. The man he'd fallen in love with was usually quiet, thoughtful and rather timid. Using the beer to wash it down, Hearn finally swallowed the mouthful of food. "You trying to kill me?" he joked, taking in every inch of the smaller man's nudity.

Tyler took a drink from his own bottle before setting it on the table. "Nope. I'm trying to revive you." He straddled Hearn's lap. "Is it working?" Tyler asked, hand kneading Hearn's erection through his jeans.

"Oh, it's working." Hearn finished off his beer in one long drink before handing the empty bottle to Tyler.

Tyler leaned backward, stretching his slim body to place the bottle on the table. Hearn took full advantage of the position by running his hands over the smooth torso in his lap.

Instead of straightening, Tyler scooted his ass against Hearn's cock and draped himself over the front of the sofa. *Damn.* Tyler was not only sexy as shit but limber as well. The new position left Tyler fully exposed to Hearn's eyes and hands.

"Am I dreaming?" Hearn asked, following the thin line of hair from Tyler's belly button to his hardening cock.

"If so, do me a favour and don't wake up," Tyler purred as Hearn's hand encircled his erection.

Hearn felt completely wicked as he used his other hand to fondle Tyler's balls. Here he sat, fully dressed, while a smorgasbord lounged on his lap. He spent his time, feeling each ridge and dip of Tyler's body.

By the time the pizza was well and truly cold, the only area he hadn't fondled was the sweet ass pressed against his stomach. Placing his hands under Tyler's back, Hearn easily lifted the man back into a seated position. "Hang on to me," he said, standing.

Tyler did as he was told and wrapped his arms and legs around Hearn. "What about the pizza?" Tyler whispered, licking Hearn's ear.

"I've always been the kind of guy who preferred to indulge in dessert before dinner." On the way to the raised Queen-sized bed, Hearn stopped by the door. "Can ya grab that bag for me?"

Tyler reached down and scooped up the small duffle. "I hope you bought enough condoms."

As Hearn carried his naked lover to bed, he began to worry. It had been quite a few years since he'd topped because Mitch had rarely let him take the lead in their love making. He hoped the few odd times he'd been allowed to penetrate his ex had given him enough experience to satisfy Tyler.

It wasn't that he hadn't enjoyed taking the lead. To the contrary, Hearn had always felt he was more a top than a bottom, but it hadn't really been a choice given to him in the past. He'd loved Mitch enough to do whatever it took to feel close to the man, at least for a while.

After walking up the three steps to the large platform, Hearn gently laid Tyler in the centre of the bed. Starting with his shirt, he quickly removed his clothes before retrieving the large box of condoms from his bag.

Tyler used the time to ogle Hearn and push the covers down to the foot of the bed. "I can't believe how amazingly gorgeous you are," Tyler groaned, reaching for the bottle of lube in the bedside drawer.

Hearn glanced down at himself. He knew his body was in good shape, playing every sport available in Cattle Valley helped with that, but he'd never thought of himself as gorgeous. If he was, wouldn't Mitch have resisted the temptation to wander? Had he been naïve? Had all the years he'd spent with Mitch been about a stupid trust fund that he didn't even have yet? Hell, unless his family forgave him, he may never have it.

The thought went a long way to cooling his desires. Tyler's hand wrapped around Hearn's softening cock. "What's wrong?" Tyler asked.

Still standing beside the bed, Hearn looked into Tyler's eyes. "Do you think Mitch ever really loved me?"

Tyler seemed surprised by the question, but he quickly schooled his features and pulled Hearn down on the bed beside him. "I think he probably loved you as much as he was capable of, at least in the beginning. Later..." Tyler shrugged, "...who knows. I refuse to defend a guy who fucked anything that moved when he had a partner like you waiting at home. But I'd like to think he gave you a little of what you deserved."

"I'm not rich. I don't know why Mitch thought I ever would be," Hearn said, shaking his head. "My family has money, but before Mitch's death they hadn't spoken to me since college." He realised something. "Mitch was constantly on my ass. Trying to get me to call and make up with them." God, it suddenly made sense. The thought of Mitch stringing him along in order to get his hands on the Sutherland millions made him laugh.

"Hearn?" Tyler put a concerned hand to Hearn's face.

"The joke was on him. My family didn't cut me off because I was gay. They cut me off because they hated Mitch. They thought he was a leach who would bleed me dry in no time."

"How do you know that?" Tyler asked.

"Because I finally took his advice and called them after he died." He still hadn't gone to see his folks, but he'd spoken with his mother and sister at least once a week since Mitch's death.

Tyler pushed him down to lie on the bed and curled his body around Hearn. "I hate to sound like a selfish prick, but can we shelve the Mitch talk for a few hours?"

Ashamed of himself for thinking about another man, when he had the one he loved naked in his arms, Hearn nodded. "Sorry."

"Don't be. I want you to know I'm here for you. It's good you're working through these things, but it feels like I've waited a lifetime to get you in bed."

Extracting all thoughts of family and Mitch from his mind, Hearn gave himself over to the moment as Tyler's hands began to wander his body. Tyler kissed his way down Hearn's face and neck as he rolled on top of him.

Hearn closed his eyes and moaned, as Tyler's skilful tongue licked its way down to the crown of his cock. "I love your dick," Tyler mumbled around said dick.

"And it evidently loves you," Hearn replied, feeling his erection return within seconds. Fuck, Tyler knew how to suck cock. Once again Hearn was amazed he'd never known this side of the timid florist.

Hearn reached over and grabbed the box of condoms. "Need to fuck you," he panted, afraid he'd come too early.

Tyler slid his mouth from Hearn's cock and reached for the lube. As Hearn struggled with the foil package, Tyler wasted no time in preparing his own hole. The scene playing out in front of him threatened his control once again. With only one prior lover, Hearn had never witnessed anything like the sight of Tyler stretching himself. "Goddamn!"

He leaned over and bit the small butt cheek that was pushed up in the air, getting a nice view of the three thin fingers thrusting in and out of Tyler's hole. The expression of ecstasy on Tyler's face spoke volumes. "You do this often?" Hearn wondered.

"Have to." Tyler removed his fingers and smiled. "I haven't had a lover since moving here."

Hearn knelt behind Tyler and pressed the head of his cock to the stretched opening. "I won't last long," he warned, before slowly pushing inside.

"Uhhhh," Tyler growled, as Hearn rocked in to the root.

The outer muscles may have been nicely loosened, but Tyler's inner muscles were squeezing Hearn's cock like a vise. *Shit, shit shit.* Hearn tried to calm his breathing. Even the few times he'd been allowed to mount Mitch hadn't prepared him for the feel of Tyler's body.

With his hands on Tyler's hips, Hearn withdrew before plunging in again. His mind wanted to take their first coupling slow, but his cock had other ideas. Before he knew it, he was ramming Tyler's ass to the audible delight of his lover. He was pleasantly surprised when Tyler howled his approaching orgasm.

"I'm coming!" Tyler yelled.

The increased pressure to his cock as Tyler's body shook with contractions sent Hearn hurtling over the edge into pure bliss. He pushed Tyler down on the bed and buried himself as deep as possible. His cock erupted, shooting its seed into the condom, as he attached his mouth to the back of Tyler's neck.

Hearn's body continued to shake with aftershocks as he came down from the most intense orgasm of his life.

"Mitch was a fucking fool," Tyler mumbled, face pressed into the pillow.

* * * *

"What do you mean, you have to tell us the truth about who you are?" Ryan asked, his hold on Nate tightening.

Nate tried to bury his face against Ryan's chest to escape his partner's suspicious eyes. Having none of it, Ryan pulled back and tilted Nate's chin up. "Nate," Ryan warned. "What's going on?"

Nate didn't know what to say. Was he about to make the biggest mistake of his life? What if the men he loved couldn't forgive him?

"Rio! Get up here!" Ryan screamed, leading Nate out of the closet.

Within moments, Rio came rushing through the doorway. "What's wrong?" he asked, looking from Ryan to Nate.

"Nate has something he needs to tell us," Ryan informed.

It was the concern in Rio's eyes that pushed Nate to do the right thing. "Sit down," he told his men.

"Nate?" Rio asked, appearing more frightened than angry.

Nate gestured to the bed. "Just give me a second."

After Rio and Ryan did as they were asked, Nate went back into the closet. He picked up the birth certificate and the envelope containing Joseph's picture.

When he returned to the bedroom, Ryan and Rio had their arms around each other, whispering softly. Taking a deep breath, Nate sat in the centre of the bed, waiting for his men to turn and face him.

"Let me start by telling you both how sorry I am. I never meant to deceive either of you, and what I'm about to explain is something I've never spoken to anyone about. It's a time in my life that I'm not proud of. Something I've spent years trying to forget, but I can't anymore."

"Just tell us for Christ's sake!" Ryan barked.

The first thing Nate did was to hand Ryan his birth certificate. "That's my birth name."

"William Nathaniel Guillome," Ryan read. He glanced from the paper, over to Rio and finally to Nate. "I don't understand."

Nate swallowed around the lump in his throat. "My father made me legally change my name after I graduated from high school. Of course that was also when he gave me a nice fat check and warned me to never darken his doorstep again."

"Why would a father do that?" Rio questioned.

"To protect the family name," Nate admitted. "He was, and still is, afraid of scandal."

"Guillome," Ryan whispered. "As in Senator William Guillome?"

"Yep," Nate confirmed. "So you can see why not only having a gay son, but one who was as open as I was would be a problem. But that's not the real reason he cut me out of his life. I made the mistake of falling in love with a fourth year Catholic seminary student."

"A priest?" Rio asked. "I didn't even know you were Catholic."

"I'm not. At least not anymore. Joseph was the son of one of our parish big wigs. I first met him when he was home for Christmas break from the university. Of course being a horny sixteen-year-old at the time, I was immediately attracted to the piece of forbidden fruit. Joseph didn't seem to return my attraction, but he did welcome my friendship. After he went back to seminary, we continued to write back and forth for the next year. During the fall of my senior year everything changed. Joseph's letters became more intimate, telling me he often thought of me before he went to sleep at night. That year when he came home for winter break, he allowed me to kiss him for the first time. One thing led to another, and I took his virginity."

"Fuck," Rio gasped.

"Yeah," Nate agreed. "I was seventeen and a half and thought I'd found my soul mate. But unfortunately Joseph obviously hadn't felt the same. He had a mini-breakdown of sorts. The guilt over what he'd done seemed to eat him alive until he finally threw himself on the mercy of his family and his priest. The priest called my father, who couldn't bring himself to look me in the eye afterward. My father told me Joseph had been sent away, and that I was to never again contact him. The afternoon of my graduation, William Guillome presented me with the check I told you about and laid out the conditions. I've not talked to him since. I moved to Chicago, changed my name and entered the police academy."

Now that the truth was finally out, Nate held his breath, waiting for a reaction from the men he loved.

Ryan's first question surprised him. "So what happens if the local press digs this up?"

"Umm, I don't know," Nate stammered. "It would ruin not only my father's career, but Joseph's as well."

"Do you care what it does to your father's career? He hasn't exactly been quiet in the press about his disapproval of 'queer folk'," Rio quipped, pulling Nate onto his lap.

The simple action was what Nate had been waiting for. He knew at least Rio wasn't ready to walk away from him. Nate shrugged. "I took his money. I may do a lot of things I'm not always proud of, but going back on my word isn't one of them."

"And Joseph? Did you ever find out what happened to him?" Ryan asked, placing a hand on Nate's back.

Nate shook his head. "I never tried. I'd already done enough harm." Nate gazed into Ryan's eyes. "I really did love him. Even after all these years, there's a part of me that still does."

Nate reached over and took the picture out of the envelope and handed it to Ryan. "Today was the first time since I met the two of you that I've looked at this."

Ryan studied the photograph for a few moments before passing it to Rio. "Good-looking guy."

"Yeah, he was," Nate agreed.

Ryan next picked up the forgotten birth certificate. "You have to submit this with the application to run, don't you?"

"Yes. That's why I'm thinking maybe it would be a better idea if I didn't. I called Carol, but she said the guidelines were pretty straight forward."

Ryan nodded. He took the photo from Rio and carefully placed both pieces of paper on the bedside table. "I'll do some research. See if I can find a loophole in the guidelines."

"So you forgive me?" Nate asked.

Ryan cupped Nate's face as Rio held him tighter. "It's not up to us to forgive your past. Have you ever lied to us?"

"No," Nate shook his head. "But I didn't tell you everything either."

Ryan leaned in and gave Nate a soft kiss. "We all have skeletons that we keep to ourselves."

"Do you?" Nate asked.

"Of course. But none of them have anything to do with how much I love you or Rio."

Nate realised the big man holding him had spoken very little. Pressing his cheek against Rio's, Nate whispered. "Do you still love me?"

"With everything that I am," Rio whispered back.

Chapter Five

After playing his part in consoling Nate, Rio passed his lover off to Ryan. "I'll go finish getting dinner on the table," he said, excusing himself. The truth was, he needed a few minutes to himself.

The fact that Nate had hid his birth name wasn't the issue for him. It was the simple truth that his lover had felt the need to do it in the first place. What kind of monster put his own political career above the life of his son?

Adding the finishing touches to his tuna casserole, Rio popped the dish into the oven. All he could think about was extracting revenge on the Senator. But how could he do that and not hurt Nate's first lover in the process?

"Shit!" he spat, realising what he needed to do. Finding Joseph wouldn't be the hard part, it was telling Joseph why he'd come that would. He heard the thump of the bed upstairs and grinned. It sounded like Ryan was doing a damn fine job of getting Nate's mind off his troubles.

With Nate taken care of and the casserole in the oven, Rio powered up his laptop. The fact that Nate still professed to love the guy made Rio uneasy. "Right is right," he mumbled to himself. The best thing he could do to help the man he loved, was to find Joseph, talk to him and let the chips fall where they may.

By the time the oven timer sounded, Rio had all the information he needed. What would his men say if he left town for a day? Maybe he should at least tell Ryan? He shut down the laptop, sticking the piece of paper with a hastily scribbled address into his pocket.

"Dinner's ready!" he yelled up the stairs, before setting the table.

He heard Nate's famous giggle seconds before the men walked into the kitchen. "I'm starved," Nate declared.

After setting the casserole in the centre of the table, Rio took his seat. "I don't doubt it with all the noise the two of you were making up there."

Ryan and Nate exchanged heated glances. "You should've joined us," Ryan crooned.

"What, and burn dinner like Nate did?" he joked, knowing it was a sore spot.

"Hardy har har," Nate replied. "I'll take Ryan's cock up my ass over a burned casserole any day."

Rio grinned. He loved the way Nate's mood was able to bounce back so quickly. It was definitely part of the smaller man's charm, a character trait that would definitely win him the mayoral election.

He decided to corner Ryan the following day and discuss his intentions. Hopefully Ryan would understand Rio's need to talk to Joseph. Even without the election, knowing there was a man out there that still held a piece of Nate's heart was reason enough. Now the truth was out in the open, Rio felt all four of them needed closure.

* * * *

Tyler opened his eyes to a greasy pizza box still on the edge of the bed. How the hell had that stayed up here? He remembered very distinctly Hearn making love to him twice after they'd taken a short dinner break.

"Mmmm, you awake?" Hearn whispered, running his hand over Tyler's hip.

"Yep. Just laying here contemplating the mysteries of the universe." Tyler turned over to face his new lover. "How did you sleep?" he asked, scraping his teeth across Hearn's stubbled chin.

"Better than I have in years." Hearn gave Tyler a kiss. "Thanks to you."

Hearn's fingers drifted down the crack of Tyler's ass. *Fuck.* Tyler flinched at the touch. "Sorry. Guess I'm a little sore."

Hearn withdrew his hand. "Don't be sorry. I'm the one who couldn't get enough of this sweet body of yours."

Tyler rolled on top of Hearn. "I think we're both guilty of that." He began peppering kisses to Hearn's face and neck. "I have to go down and open the shop," he said between kisses. "What're your plans?"

"Mmm," Hearn moaned, tilting his chin up. "To enjoy this for as long as I can. Then I'll go to the Centre after dropping the paperwork off at City Hall."

Tyler stopped what he was doing and sat up. "So you're really gonna do it?"

"Run for mayor? Yeah. I thought I'd toss my name in the mix."

"I know a great place that'll do your signs. I'd suggest a quality plastic that'll hold up in the weather." He knew it was a huge step for Hearn. Hopefully, with a little encouragement, Hearn would break free of the shell he'd placed himself in. Tyler couldn't blame him. Hearing the person you love constantly cut you down would lower anyone's self-esteem.

"Hell, I didn't even think of that. To be honest, I'm not sure what's involved in running for office."

Hearing the worry and self-doubt in Hearn's voice, broke Tyler's heart. "Well, we'll put up signs of course, and then you'll probably have to speak at a town meeting. Ya know, talk about what you'll do as mayor and stuff. Everyone in town already knows you, so just try and make a concerted effort to speak to people on the streets and in stores." He leaned down and gave Hearn a deep kiss. "You'll do great."

"Do you think people will whisper about Mitch behind my back? I don't want to put myself out there if it's going to cause you embarrassment."

"It won't," Tyler whispered. "And that's exactly the reason I fell in love with you. No matter what else is going on, you always put other people first. It's the reason you'll make a great mayor. Besides, you've done absolutely nothing wrong. If people want to talk about Mitch, let them, but the only crime you've committed is loving an asshole."

"I hope you're right," Hearn mumbled.

Tyler ran his hand down Hearn's perfect six-pack. "Do you think sometime I could go to the Centre with you?"

"Seriously? You'd go?"

"I love kids," Tyler stated, hurt that Hearn would think otherwise.

"It's just, you know, a lot of the kids have problems. They aren't the perfectly healthy children that people want to adopt. It bugs some people to be around 'em."

Is that what he really thinks of me? Tyler slid off the bed. "I'm gonna grab a quick shower. There's some juice in the fridge if you want some."

Shutting the door to the only contained room in his loft, Tyler studied himself in the mirror. Why had he reacted so strongly to Hearn's words? His father's hateful words drifted back to him.

"Why couldn't I have had a real boy instead of you? Someone I could at least play catch with. But no, I had to get stuck with a pussy boy. No real man would want a son like you."

Tyler closed his eyes and tried to push the image of his dad's enraged face out of his mind. He'd made the mistake of trying to block his dad's fist from connecting with his mom's jaw and had gotten it instead.

The bathroom door suddenly opened, jarring Tyler from his memories. Hearn leaned against the door jam with his arms crossed over his chest. "Mind telling me what just happened in there?"

Tyler turned away and started the shower. "Just need to get on with my day."

Hearn stepped between Tyler and the shower stall. "It's more than that and we both know it. If I said something wrong, I'm sorry." Hearn put his hands on his hips and gazed at the floor. "Mitch gave me a hard time about visiting the Centre. I didn't go much when he was alive for that reason. It just surprised me that you'd be interested. I didn't mean to hurt your feelings."

Knowing he'd made too much of it already, Tyler wrapped his arms around Hearn's waist and squeezed. "No. I'm sorry I acted like a child. It's kind of a sensitive subject."

Hearn's eyes narrowed as his head tilted to the side. "You'll need to tell me why. Otherwise, I'm likely to make the same mistake again."

Tyler wasn't ready to get into his screwed-up childhood just yet. Instead, he leaned in and bit Hearn's dark brown nipple. "We're wasting all the hot water."

Hearn reached behind him and reopened the shower door. He took a step backwards under the spray, bringing Tyler with him. With the hot water raining down on them, Tyler's hands began to roam Hearn's muscular body.

"Are you trying to distract me?" Hearn chuckled.

"Is it working?" Tyler kissed his way down Hearn's body. If it weren't for his sore ass, he'd bend over and let the bigger man fuck him right there.

Hearn put his hands on Tyler's shoulders and guided him to the floor. "As you can see, it's working quite nicely."

Tyler ran his tongue around the twin orbs hanging underneath Hearn's erection, taking first one and then the other into his mouth. Hearn rewarded him with a moan and a slight thrust of his hips.

Feeling much better than he had a few moments earlier, Tyler licked his way up Hearn's length to slip over the rosy crown. He used one hand to wrap around the base of Hearn's cock while his other fisted his own.

Hearn took his hand from Tyler's head to readjust the shower spray. "Look at me," Hearn panted, as Tyler bobbed back and forth on his cock.

With the spray out of his face, Tyler peered up the length of Hearn's body. The heavy-lidded gaze of his lover stared back at him. "Come with me," Hearn groaned.

Moving his hands in tandem, Tyler took as much of Hearn's length as he could and nodded. Surprise registered on Hearn's face as he shot the first volley of seed down Tyler's throat.

"Fuck!" Hearn howled, fisting Tyler's hair.

The taste of Hearn's cum combined with the hand brutally jerking his cock, pushed Tyler over the edge. The orgasm so intense, he was forced to let Hearn's cock slip from his mouth in order to breathe.

After several moments, Hearn reached down and helped Tyler to his feet. "Amazing," Hearn whispered, bending down for a deep kiss.

Tyler opened fully to Hearn's questing tongue, readily sharing the man's own essence with him. How could he ever think this man would look down on him for anything? Hearn was still the kindest man he'd ever known, and one hell of a lover. He grinned.

"So will ya?" Hearn asked, breaking their kiss.

"Will I what?" *Did I miss something?*

"I asked you to come with me," Hearn replied.

Tyler chuckled and began shampooing his hair. "I just did."

Hearn appeared confused for several seconds before laughing. "I meant will you come with me to the Centre, though the other was quite nice, too."

"Better than nice, and I'd love to go with you." Tyler nudged Hearn out of the way and rinsed himself off.

"Great. Just tell me when you can get away." Hearn waited for Tyler to finish before stepping under the spray.

"How about now? Business has been for shit lately anyway. I'll just put a sign up in the window saying I'll be back this afternoon."

Finished, Hearn shut the water off. "I want to stop by City Hall and drop off the papers first. Would you like to go with me or wait here?"

Tyler shrugged, and handed Hearn a towel. "I'll go."

Hearn rubbed himself quickly and hung the towel over the shower stall. "You're gonna fall in love with Gracie. I can't wait for you to meet her."

"Did you bring the lamb with you?" Tyler asked, stepping into his underwear.

"It's in the truck." Hearn rummaged around in his bag and pulled out clean clothes.

Hearn started to say something but stopped. Tyler could tell by his lover's expression something bothered him. "What's wrong?"

"Nothing," Hearn denied. "Feel like grabbing some breakfast to go at Deb's?"

"Why don't I do that while you take care of your paperwork? It'll save us time and the food will still be hot by the time we're on the road to Sheridan." Tyler had a strong feeling he knew what was on Hearn's mind. He resolved to tell his lover everything about his past, just not right now.

* * * *

Rio knocked on the open door. "You got a minute?"

Ryan glanced up from his computer and smiled. "For you? Always."

With a returning grin, Rio stepped into the office and shut the door. Before taking a seat, he stopped to give his partner a kiss. "How's your morning?"

Ryan gave Rio one last swipe of his tongue before pulling back. "Well, I've only been here for an hour, but so far I can't complain. Although we're expecting another storm, so ask me again later."

"Yeah, I heard that on the radio on my way over," Rio commented, taking a seat.

"So...what can I do for you?" Ryan asked.

"I found him," Rio simply stated.

"Where?" Ryan leaned forward with his forearms on the desk.

"DC."

Ryan blew out an exasperated breath and leaned back in his chair. "So, he never left."

Rio shook his head. "I booked a ten o'clock flight," he confessed.

His partner's eyes narrowed. "Why?"

"Cuz I need to know and I think you do, too." He crossed his arms, prepared for an argument.

Ryan's attention shifted to the window beside his desk. After several long moments, he nodded. "He either doesn't know Nate's new name or doesn't care. Why dredge it all up again? What if he wants him back?"

Rio stood and went to Ryan's side. "That's exactly the reason I'm going to DC. I can't spend the rest of my life afraid some old love is gonna come out of the woodwork. I've always met trouble head on, and I think this guy may be just that."

"What about the Senator? What if he finds out?" Ryan asked.

"The Senator isn't my problem. I don't give a fuck about him. Although to be honest, I wouldn't mind taking the bigoted prick down a few notches, but that's not up to me. My main concern is Nate, and the fact that there's a man out there that still holds a piece of him. A man with whom our partner has unfinished business."

Ryan stood and pulled Rio into his arms. "What'll you tell Nate?"

"I won't. I can't lie to him, and if I tell him he'll just insist on going with me. Hopefully by the time he realises I'm gone, I'll have already talked to Joseph."

Ryan grinned. "Come on, it's Nate. He'll realise your gone by noon when he's looking for a little action."

Rio ran his hand down Ryan's chest to press against his lover's cock. "I guess you need to be there to distract him then."

A coal black brow shot up. "That could work. As a matter of fact, the idea sounds so good that I may just have to take an early lunch."

Rio could feel Ryan's cock hardening in his hand. "Go get 'em, tiger."

Ryan pulled Rio's head down for a deep kiss. "When'll you be home?"

"Not sure. It depends on Joseph and what he has to say."

"Call me. Let me know what's going on. I'll try to keep Nate…occupied."

Chuckling, Rio squeezed his partner's erection. "I just bet you will."

* * * *

The first flakes of snow were beginning to fall when Hearn pulled up in front of the old brick building. "How many kids live here?" Tyler asked.

Hearn put the truck into park and turned off the engine. "Right now there's fourteen, but they're trying to get a couple of them placed into foster care. They're really only set up to house twelve."

Tyler leaned across the seat and gave Hearn a quick kiss. He could tell his lover was nervous about bringing him.

This was a side of himself that Hearn usually kept private, and Tyler knew what a privilege it was to be invited in. The last thing he would do was embarrass the sweet man in any way. He reached down and picked up the lavender bag containing the stuffed animal. "Ready?"

Hearn took the bag out of Tyler's hand and pulled the lamb out. After placing the toy inside his jacket, he winked. "Don't want the other kids to get jealous. I'll wait and give this to Gracie once we're alone."

"Good idea," Tyler agreed. He hadn't even thought about bringing enough for everyone. "Next time, we'll bring more."

With a dazzling smile firmly in place, Hearn clutched the front of Tyler's coat and kissed him again. "I love you," Hearn whispered against Tyler's lips.

Even though Hearn had spoken much the same thing before, the words still excited him. He rolled his eyes and sat back in his seat. "Great. Now I've got an erection big enough to scare the children."

Hearn chuckled and ran his hand over the fly of Tyler's jeans. "Not helping," Tyler reminded him, trying to arrange a funeral bouquet in his head. "You go ahead. I'll just stand out in the snow for a few minutes."

Still laughing, Hearn got out of the truck. Tyler watched the man's gorgeous ass as it disappeared through the front door. With his cock still painfully hard, Tyler got out of the truck. He had been right. Within a few moments, his erection had softened enough to be presentable.

He stepped inside the front door and spotted Hearn talking to the receptionist. "Everything okay?" Hearn asked, giving him a wink.

"For now," he answered.

Hearn motioned him over. "Beth, I'd like you to meet my boyfriend, Tyler."

Boyfriend? Tyler wanted to giggle. He'd been referred to as a good fuck or a one-night stand kind-of-guy, but never a boyfriend. *I like it.*

Tyler extended his hand to the older woman behind the desk. "Very nice to meet you."

"You, too. Are you the florist I've heard Hearn mention?"

Tyler looked at Hearn. "You've mentioned me?"

Hearn shrugged and pointed towards the clipboard. "You need to sign in."

Seeing the red flush on Hearn's cheeks, Tyler dropped the subject and did as asked. Setting the pen back in its holder, he took his lover's hand. "Ready?"

Hearn dropped a quick kiss on Tyler's forehead. "I'd like to introduce Gracie to Tyler. Is she in her room?" Hearn asked Beth.

"Should be," Beth answered, glancing down at a paper in front of her.

"Thanks," Hearn said. "Come on."

Tyler let Hearn lead him by the hand through a door into a big open room. Though the furniture appeared worn and mismatching, the room had a familial appearance to it. "This the living room?"

"Yep. It's where the kids play and watch television."

Tyler could tell the Centre did their best to give the children a sense of home. "Nice."

Hearn led him through another door and down a short hall. A sudden attack of nerves hit Tyler. He planted his feet and tugged on Hearn's hand until his lover stopped and looked at him. "What if she doesn't like me?"

Hearn wrapped his arms around Tyler. "How could she not? You're everything good in the world rolled into a little ball of sunshine."

Is that how Hearn saw him? Although the sentiment was beautiful, Tyler didn't know that he deserved it. He thought about contradicting his lover, but bit his tongue instead. They were there to see Gracie, not get into Tyler's true psyche. Taking a deep breath, he nodded. "Okay, I'm ready."

Chapter Six

"Looking good, Asa," Nate observed, walking up to the wealthiest man in town.

Asa Montgomery picked up his towel and mopped his face and neck. "I ought to. I've been busting my ass lately."

Nate grinned. He'd noticed Asa had picked up another kick-boxing lesson with Mario. Asa was in his mid-forties, but you'd never know it by the solid muscles visible under the tight navy T-shirt. "Is Mario being too hard on you?"

"Actually, I think he's slowly working me into the best shape of my life. He's a demanding sonofabitch, I'll give him that."

"Good to know." Nate spotted Ryan's SUV pulling up in front of the window. "Sorry, Asa, but my man's here."

Asa chuckled and waved Nate off. "Go have fun while you're still young."

Nate started to turn, but stopped and addressed Asa. "You're only as old as you feel, especially if you can get someone younger to feel ya." He winked and turned to greet his partner.

"This is a nice surprise," Nate said, pouncing on Ryan as soon as he walked through the door.

Ryan shook the snow out of his hair and wrapped his arms around Nate. "Well, I figured it was about that time of day, and I know Rio is off on an errand."

Nate pulled Ryan's head down for a kiss. "You two know me so well. Let's go into the office."

After closing the door behind them, Nate led Ryan to the wide couch. "I made reservations for the two of us at Canoe later."

Nate paused in stripping off his clothes. "The two of us? Why? Where'd Rio go that he won't be back in time for dinner?"

When Ryan didn't say anything and suddenly refused to look at him, Nate knew something was going on. "Ryan? Where's Rio?"

Ryan began unbuttoning his uniform shirt. "On an errand."

Nate put his hands on Ryan's face and forced his lover to make eye contact. "Where's Rio?" he repeated the question. He knew Ryan wouldn't lie to him if he could just get past Ryan's stubborn need to protect their partner.

"DC," Ryan finally mumbled.

Nate released Ryan and took a step back. He felt as though he'd just been punched. "Why would he do that?" All he could think about was Rio going after his father.

Ryan took a deep breath and squared his shoulders. "He found Joseph."

Nate felt the burn of impending tears sting his eyes. *Joseph?* Images of his heavily muscled lover confronting the gentle man he'd once known scared him. "Give me the address," Nate demanded, putting his shoes back on.

"I can't," Ryan whispered, studying the floor.

"More like you won't," Nate accused. "If Rio's gone there to hurt Joseph in any way I'll never forgive either of you."

"It's not like that," Ryan spat.

"It's not like what?"

Ryan's gaze moved to Nate's, tears shimmering in his eyes. Having never seen his lover cry, Nate was completely floored. "Ryan?" he prompted.

"He's...we're afraid of losing you. Rio went to see what Joseph's feelings are towards you."

Seeing the obvious worry in his partner's face, Nate couldn't retain his anger. *Dammit.* He should've never told them about Joseph. Taking the few steps that separated them, Nate wrapped his arms around Ryan. "You're not gonna lose me."

"You can't promise that. Up until now, you didn't know where Joseph was."

"Because I didn't try," Nate reminded him. "I was a private detective for Christ's sake. I could've found Joseph if I'd really wanted to, but he'd already made his choice."

"He's not a priest," Ryan admitted. "He runs a non-denominational church in the heart of DC."

Nate's heart skipped a beat at the news. Had Joseph tried to find him? "Will you go with me to DC?"

Ryan hugged him closer. "I can't, not now. With the storm blowing in and Quade no longer at the helm, George is gonna need all the help he can get." Ryan rested his head against Nate's. "I wish I could, believe me."

"I do," Nate consoled. "But I need to go. I need to say goodbye to Joseph."

Ryan nodded. "I know, baby."

* * * *

Holding hands, Tyler followed Hearn into Gracie's room. "Hey there, princess," Hearn greeted the little girl.

A small dark-haired girl peered up from her doll and smiled. "Hearn!" she squealed, jumping up from the floor and running towards the big man.

Her gaze suddenly swung to Tyler and she skidded to a stop two feet away. The expression of fear on her face broke Tyler's heart.

"Don't be afraid," Hearn cajoled, kneeling on the floor to get down to Gracie's level. "This is my boyfriend, Tyler. He wanted to meet the girl who means so much to me."

Gracie stood her ground, eyeing Tyler warily. He couldn't help but notice the thin scar running down the pretty little girl's cheek. *Had her mother done that?* Once again he felt ashamed of himself. Although his dad had hit him, he'd never done anything to permanently scar Tyler. From the looks of it, he'd had a good life compared to Gracie.

Not wanting to frighten the girl further, Tyler took several steps back. "I can wait for you in the reception area," he said.

"No," Hearn said, reaching back for Tyler's hand. Hearn turned his attention back to the frightened girl. "Remember we talked about the difference between good people and bad people?"

Gracie's gaze swung from Tyler back to Hearn. She nodded slowly.

"Well, Tyler's one of the good people. As a matter of fact, I think he's the best person I've ever known, and he means an awful lot to me. Do you understand?" he asked in a gentle fashion.

After several tense moments, Gracie stepped forward and held out her tiny hand. "I'm Gracie."

Swallowing around the newly-formed lump in his throat, Tyler shook the girl's hand. "Nice to meet you, Gracie. Hearn's told me a lot about you."

Gracie smiled at the news before wrapping her arms around Hearn's neck. "I missed you."

"I missed you, too, princess." He leaned back and put his hand inside his jacket. "Look here what we brought for you." Hearn pulled out the white lamb. "It came from Tyler's store. He owns a flower shop in Cattle Valley."

Gracie's entire face lit up as she hugged the animal to her chest. "He's so cute."

Her little body twisted back and forth as she continued to hug the cheap stuffed animal. Suddenly Tyler wanted to fill the room with as many toys as it would hold.

Hearn chuckled, standing to put his arm around Tyler's waist. "I think she likes it."

"I'll say," Tyler agreed.

"Wanna have a tea party?" Gracie asked, gazing up at them.

Tyler noticed the paper cups on the floor beside her now-forgotten doll. "I think we'd love that."

With a nod, Gracie walked over and sat down. "Come on," she giggled. "You can't have tea standing up."

With a wink, Hearn released Tyler. They walked over and sat across from each other on the small thread-bare rug. Tyler marvelled at the way Gracie handled the throw-away cups, as if they were real china. He vowed to buy her a real set as soon as possible.

As Gracie handed a cup to Hearn, Tyler watched the man he loved. Hearn's entire face had taken on an unmistakable glow. *He really does love her.* Tyler wondered if Hearn had ever considered adopting a child. It was obvious the man was good with kids, and from the looks of the centre, there were plenty of children that needed homes.

They spent the next two hours enjoying their tea party and playing games. Tyler admitted defeat on more than one occasion. "I can see I'm going to have to brush up on my skills," he informed Gracie.

The little girl giggled. "Nothing wrong with losing. It's willing to play in the first place that's important."

Tyler reached out and smoothed a wayward black curl off Gracie's forehead. "How'd you get to be so wise?"

Gracie pointed to Hearn. "That's what he always tells me when I lose."

The fact that Gracie didn't pull away from the gentle touch made him feel like a king, until he made the mistake of grazing the scar with his finger.

Gracie's eyes went wide as she covered the area with her hand. "I'm sorry. I know I'm ugly."

Tyler automatically reached out, wanting to take the little girl into his arms. An interrupting cough from Hearn stopped him. Tyler glanced towards the man he loved. Hearn gave a slight shake of his head.

"That scar doesn't make you any less beautiful," Tyler tried to apologise, but the damage had apparently already been done.

Gracie turned away and hugged her lamb to her chest. Tyler glanced at Hearn pleadingly. "What do I do?" he mouthed.

In answer, Hearn stood and scooped Gracie from the floor. "Hey." Hearn bounced the sad little girl in his arms. He walked with Gracie over to the mirror and stood there. "Look at yourself."

Gracie buried her head against Hearn's neck and shook her head. "Mary Grace Cook, do as I asked," he gently reprimanded.

Tyler wiped at the tears running down his cheeks. He couldn't believe he'd just blown any chance he had of getting close to Gracie.

As he watched, Gracie slowly lifted her head and turned to regard her reflection. "What do you see?" Hearn asked.

"A scar," Gracie mumbled, sticking her bottom lip out.

"Really? Because what I see is a little girl with big blue eyes and rosy lips. Why, the only thing I see wrong is that pout on your face. How many times have we talked about this? Hmmm? True beauty comes from within, but so does ugly. Now I happen to know you're beautiful on the inside, so how can you possibly imagine you're ugly on the outside?"

Gracie didn't say anything but ran her finger down the scar from her outer eye to her chin. Hearn shook his head. "Nope. Not buying it." He touched his lips to Gracie's cheek. "If you let people see that inner beauty that I know you possess, they'll never even notice that tiny scar."

Tyler watched in awe as Gracie seemed to absorb every word Hearn said.

"You're the only one who can do that. I can tell you you're pretty every day for the rest of your life, but until you're able to truly see it, you'll never believe it, in here," he whispered, tapping her chest.

Hearn turned to Tyler and held out his hand. "Tyler didn't mean to make you feel bad. Did you, Tyler?"

"No. I wasn't even thinking of the scar when I touched you. What I really wanted was to hold you, but I didn't think you'd let me, so I touched your cheek instead."

"See there?" Hearn asked Gracie. "You've only known my boyfriend for a couple of hours and already you're trying to take him away from me."

Gracie's red lips turned into a smile before finally breaking out into a giggle. "I didn't mean to," she said with her earlier cheer. "It just happens sometimes."

Hearn pulled Tyler against them. Gracie reached out and wrapped one arm around Tyler's neck, still leaving one around Hearn's and hugged them both. Tyler followed suit, as did Hearn.

After feeling the little girl in his arms for the first time, Tyler knew his life would never be the same.

* * * *

Nate stepped out of the airport and called Rio's phone. He was sure Ryan had probably already called to warn him of Nate's arrival, but he'd yet to speak with his wayward lover.

"You here?" Rio answered.

"Yep. Where're you?"

"The Hyatt on H Street."

"Have you seen him?" Nate asked, getting into a cab. "Hyatt on H," he told the driver before returning his attention to Rio.

"No. Ryan called right after I landed, so I got a room instead."

Nate could tell by the sound of his lover's voice that he wasn't happy. *Well too bad.* "It's getting late. We might do better to meet with Joseph in the morning."

"He's already expecting us. I called him earlier. I thought it only fair to warn him you were coming," Rio answered in a clipped fashion.

"What room are you in?"

"Five-fourteen."

Frustrated with their stilted conversation, Nate sighed. "Fine. I'll be there in a few." He hung up the phone and looked out the passenger window. It had been years since he'd stepped foot in DC. He briefly thought about calling his mom. Would she even dare to see him? They'd had a few phone calls over the years, but they were always short and in secret.

The closer he came to the hotel, the tighter his stomach clenched. He wasn't sure what to say to Rio when he saw him. He was still pissed his partner would take off without telling him, but he also knew he'd have done the same thing. The bigger question was why Rio sounded so pissed when they'd spoken?

Nate was known for his ability to charm the bigger man, but would anything he had to say do the trick this time? *Wait a minute. Why am I worried about easing Rio's mood? I'm not the one who ran off to DC half-cocked.*

The cab pulled up outside the Hyatt, and Nate pressed several bills into the driver's hand. He grabbed his overnight bag from the seat beside him and entered the grand hotel. The elevator ride was reasonably short, and before he knew it, Nate stood outside room five-fourteen. He gave the door an even handed knock and waited.

Rio opened immediately, stepping back to let Nate enter.

"Before you start yelling at me, let me explain," Rio said.

Now that Nate was in Rio's presence, he realised it wasn't anger, but hurt that prompted the short answers earlier. Dropping his bag to the floor, Nate launched himself into Rio's arms. He'd somehow managed to hurt the two people he loved most in the world. "Seeing Joseph isn't worth hurting you," Nate told his lover.

Rio seemed surprised by Nate's statement. "What? You'd come all this way and not talk to him?"

Nate didn't even need to consider the question. "Yes, if that's what you want." He framed Rio's face with his hands. "I won't lie and say I'm not curious, but not for the reason you think."

"You told us you loved him," Rio mumbled.

"I told you a part of me still loves him, it's not the same as what I feel for you and Ryan. I'm not in love with Joseph. He was always the loose end of my life left dangling out there. Now that we're here, maybe I can finally close that chapter of my life."

"I saw his picture on the internet. He's even more handsome than that photograph you still have."

Nate grinned. "Excuse me? Have you ever looked in the mirror?" Nate ran his hands over Rio's broad chest. "Does he have pecs to die for? Does he have dimples I love to kiss?" He gave Rio a kiss. "Can he make me feel loved simply by smiling at me?"

Nate shook his head. "I was a boy when I fell in love with Joseph. I hate to admit it, but that was a very long time ago. Believe me, Rio, there's nothing Joseph could ever say or do to make me want him over what I already have. You're stuck with me."

Rio smiled. "In that case, I think we have time for a shower before meeting him downstairs for dinner."

Chapter Seven

Nate tucked the white collar under his camel coloured cashmere sweater and turned to Rio. His partner leaned against the door, arms crossed, dressed to die for. If he'd done nothing else to improve his lovers lives at least he'd taught them to dress well. Of course it helped when they let him buy most of their clothes.

Wearing the black pants and shirt Nate had bought him for Christmas, Rio looked...dangerous. The long-sleeved silk blend shirt moulded to his lover's chest, defining each ridge and dip. The overly-long mop of black curls Nate loved to run his hands through was secured in a leather thong at his nape. "You are one sexy motherfucker."

The corner of Rio's mouth lifted in a boyish grin. "Can't have you getting all tempted by this preacher man," Rio commented.

"Not gonna happen." Nate walked over to stand in front of his partner.

"Sure about that?" Rio asked.

Nate could still see the worry etched around Rio's eyes. After the fuck they'd shared in the shower, he'd hoped Rio would feel a little more confident. "See this ass?" Nate asked, turning around to present his butt. "I don't know where that little spinny-twirly thing you did came from, but I'm gonna be feeling it all through dinner."

Rio reached out and smacked Nate's ass hard. "I bought a book."

Surprised, Nate spun around, rubbing his ass. "You bought a book?"

Rio rolled his eyes. "I can read ya know?"

Nate put his hand to his mouth to cover the smile. "I know, big man. So, what kind of book did you buy?"

"Sex stuff," Rio simply stated.

Nate's brows shot up. "Sex stuff?"

"Ya know…positions. Don't want things to get stale between us," Rio confessed.

With a sigh, he wrapped his arms around his lover. Nate knew what it meant for Rio to admit his insecurities. Although Rio was the quiet one of the threesome, he felt everything twice as deeply, but that didn't mean he always shared those feelings.

Instead of calling him on his admitted fears, Nate pulled Rio down for a kiss. "I love you, and I'll always want that prized dick up my ass, spinny-twirly thing or not."

Rio grinned. "Good to know."

Nate glanced at his watch. "It's time."

Rio nodded and opened the door. "After you."

After a short ride down the elevator, Rio pointed in the restaurant's direction. Nate didn't miss the proprietary hand on the small of his back. "I'm nervous," Nate confessed before entering.

"So am I," Rio admitted.

Stepping up to the host, Nate smiled. "We're meeting Joseph Allenbrand," he told the tall man.

"This way. You're party's expecting you."

The host showed them to a small room off to the side of the main dining room. Nate looked up at Rio. "Did you make the reservation?"

Rio shook his head.

The host bowed, indicating for Nate and Rio to enter the small private dining area. "Your server will be along momentarily."

After a deep breath, Nate stepped into the room. Joseph and another man stood as soon as they entered. Rio had been right. Joseph was even more handsome than he had been all those years ago. The slight hint of grey in his otherwise dark hair set off the blue in his eyes perfectly. "Joseph," Nate greeted, when his old friend stepped around the table.

"Will." Joseph returned the greeting and pulled Nate into an embrace.

Nate stepped back and studied the face he'd longed to see for years. "It's Nate now."

"Yes, of course, I'm sorry. You're partner told me that on the phone. I'm afraid it may take some getting used to."

Nate reached behind him for Rio's hand. "This is one of my partners, Rio Adega."

Rio held out his hand and Joseph took it. "One of your partners?" Joseph asked, brows rising questioningly.

Nate grinned. "Ryan's our other partner, but he couldn't get away to meet you."

Joseph nodded before turning to the man to his left. "This is Phillip, my partner."

After the introductions had been made, Joseph gestured to the table. "Please, sit down."

Nate was pleased when Rio automatically pulled his chair out for him. "Thank you," he said, gazing up at his lover. Rio took the seat next to Nate's and placed his napkin on his lap.

"So," Joseph began. "Rio tells me you're thinking of running for mayor?"

Nate glanced at Rio. His lover's slightly guilty wince almost made him laugh. "Yes," he answered, returning his attention to Joseph. "I've run into a stumbling block however. In order to register my name for consideration, I have to supply my birth certificate with the application."

Joseph nodded his head in understanding. "And you're afraid your new name will cause problems."

"For you mostly," Nate admitted. "At this point in my life I'm not sure I care about what my father thinks of anything. If the press gets wind of it and decides to go after him, so be it."

"I appreciate that," Joseph replied. "But you won't cause any trouble for me. I've found my place in this world, and I've been completely open with my small but devoted congregation."

Nate began to squirm in his chair. Rio must've noticed because his lover reached under the table to hold Nate's hand. "So, you're still a priest?" Nate asked. He felt incredibly uncomfortable asking, especially with Phillip in the room.

"Not a priest, no," Joseph answered, shaking his head. "Shortly after I was sent away, I tried to commit suicide." As Joseph spoke he pushed back his shirt to reveal the truth of his words. The long thin scars were gut wrenching. *What if Joseph had succeeded?* Would Nate have felt guilty for the rest of his life?

"I felt I'd failed not only you, but especially God. The fact that I survived helped me to understand that God had forgiven me. Unfortunately, the church hadn't. I was immediately thrown out of the seminary and sent on my way."

Nate tried unsuccessfully to cover a gasp. "I'm so sorry." He knew how strong Joseph's faith had been. To be rejected…

"Don't be," Joseph was quick to say. "I'm happier now than I could've ever been. When I arrived home, I volunteered at a free health clinic here in downtown DC. That's where I met my Phillip." He reached over and took his lover's hand. "With Phillip's help, I was able to open a small shelter next to the clinic. There are so many under-aged men on the streets whose only crime was coming out to their families. We take them in, clothe them and help them to find jobs. On Sundays, we hold worship services. So you see, I'm exactly where I need to be."

Nate sat in awe of the man to his left. Joseph had led such a productive and worthwhile life it almost shamed him. He thought of the money in his bank account. Although his father hadn't paid him off with a king's ransom, Nate had been a very savvy investor over the years. His account held more than enough to last him the rest of his life. The thought of helping to fund the shelter made him smile. His father would have a stroke if he knew his money was funding such an organisation. "I want to help."

* * * *

Tyler sat beside Hearn on the drive back to Cattle Valley. He hadn't spoken much since leaving the centre, his thoughts swirling inside his head like a tornado ripping through Kansas. "Have you ever thought of adopting Gracie?"

Hearn, whose own thoughts seemed to be keeping him busy, put a hand on Tyler's thigh. "Huh?"

Tyler chuckled. "I asked if you'd ever considered adopting Gracie."

Hearn seemed surprised at the question. "Ah, no, not really. She deserves a family."

Tyler rolled his eyes and turned sideways in the seat. "What she deserves is love, and that you have for her in spades."

Hearn gave a little shake to his head as if to clear it. "There's more to raising a kid besides loving them."

"Like what?" Tyler was curious about Hearn's views on what a real family should be.

"Well, there's clothing them, feeding them…"

"All of which you have the means to do," Tyler interrupted.

"It just wouldn't be right," Hearn stated.

Tyler knew he'd continue to work on Hearn regarding the issue. His lover had far too much love in his heart to deny the little girl they'd just left. "Will you do me a favour?"

"Sure, if I can."

"I'll drop the discussion for now if you'll promise to think about something for me. How would you feel if someone swooped in and adopted Gracie tomorrow? Would you be able to live with yourself if you never again had the chance to hold her in your arms?"

Tyler watched Hearn closely as he spoke. The pain visible on the man's face said it all. Tyler leaned over and kissed the bigger man's neck. "I'm sorry if it hurts, but it's something you need to think about before it's too late."

They drove the rest of the way to Cattle Valley in silence. With the cold chill sitting beside him, Tyler unbuckled and moved to the other side of the truck cab's bench seat. It came as quite a surprise when Hearn bypassed Tyler's shop and headed towards his house.

Pulling into the garage, Hearn shut down the engine and turned to Tyler. "Thought I'd make you some dinner if you're up for it?"

He could tell by the tone of Hearn's voice he was asking for more than just dinner. Tyler could've kicked himself. Had he unknowingly made Hearn feel like he was criticising him for not adopting Gracie? *Shit.*

Tyler released himself from the seat belt and slid across to Hearn's lap. With the steering wheel against his back, he wrapped his arms around Hearn's neck and kissed him. "I'd love to stay for dinner," he whispered.

Hearn looked like he wanted to say more, but instead simply smiled. "Spaghetti?"

"Sounds good," Tyler agreed, opening Hearn's door. He could tell something between them had shifted, but he wasn't sure if it was good or bad. He sent up a silent prayer as he waited for Hearn to climb out of the truck. *Lord, please don't let me screw this up.*

* * * *

After putting the last of the dishes in the dishwasher, Hearn turned to Tyler. "Stay over and watch a movie with me?"

Tyler nodded enthusiastically. "You do have a DVD player in your bedroom, right?"

Chuckling, Hearn turned off the kitchen light and wrapped his arm around Tyler's shoulders. "I do, as a matter of fact."

As he led Tyler over to the DVD cabinet, he continued to work through things in his mind. Tyler had been right earlier. He hadn't allowed himself to think about Gracie leaving the centre with another family. There was a large part of him that knew it would be best for her to have both a mother and a father, but Gracie was a special case. Hearn seriously doubted she'd ever get over her fear of women, and who could blame her?

The hour drive home had given him a lot of time to think. He'd realised he did want a family, but not without Tyler. Watching his lover with Gracie earlier had cemented Hearn's feelings for the man. It hadn't mattered that the two most important people in his life had hit a few speed bumps. The important thing was the hug Tyler had given Gracie before they had left. As she wrapped her little arms around Tyler's neck, Gracie had looked up at Hearn and smiled. His angel appeared truly happy right there in Tyler's embrace.

"How 'bout this one?" Tyler asked, holding up Walking Tall.

Hearn chuckled. "Are you sure? Do you know how many times I've jacked off watching The Rock in action?"

Tyler's face screwed up like he'd just sucked a lemon and put the movie back on the shelf. "I may never watch another one of his movies again."

Next, Tyler picked up the new James Bond flick. Yep, Hearn had jacked off to Daniel Craig as well, but he wasn't about to admit that to Tyler, if he did, he'd be reduced to watching nothing but animated cartoons. *Damn. I'm a pathetic horndog.*

"That's good," Hearn agreed with Tyler's choice.

Feeling only slightly guilty, Hearn pulled Tyler towards the bedroom. As Tyler loaded the movie, Hearn undressed and slid under the covers.

Tyler turned around and chuckled. "Wow, you're fast."

"I wanted to watch the pre-movie entertainment." Fluffing his pillows against the headboard, he clasped his hands and set them in his lap. "Okay, I'm ready."

Still laughing, Tyler began to shimmy and sway to unheard music. Hearn couldn't help chuckling as his lover slowly pulled the shirt over his head. He whipped the long-sleeved T-shirt above his head as if it were a lasso or something. Hearn rolled his eyes and shook his head at his partner's silliness.

Dropping the shirt to the floor, Tyler slowly unbuttoned his jeans and slid them down his legs, kicking them to the side. Once completely naked, the sultry dance turned into more of a bodybuilding routine, with Tyler flexing his toned, but small muscles this way and that.

"Hah, The Rock ain't got nothin' on me," Tyler boasted, ending the routine with a kiss to each biceps.

Although the entire show was meant to be entertaining, and it was, Hearn pointed to the tented covers at his groin. "You're right, baby, I'll never jack off to anyone but you again."

Seemingly satisfied, Tyler gave Hearn a short nod before bouncing onto the bed. "You're damn right you won't."

Lifting the blankets, Tyler moulded himself to Hearn's side. "Want a pillow?" Hearn asked, stacking another one against the headboard.

"Nope, got all I need right here." Tyler laid his head on Hearn's chest and settled in. "Okay, I'm ready," Tyler informed him.

Hearn hit the play button and tossed the remote onto the bedside table. He doubted they'd get much movie watching in, but he was willing to give it a shot.

About fifteen minutes into the film, Tyler moved his leg up to brush his knee against Hearn's half-hard erection. Hearn bit back the moan, curious as to what his little man would try next.

He didn't have to wait long, before Tyler glanced up at him. "You cold?" Tyler used it as an excuse to put the covers up around his shoulders.

"I'm good," Hearn answered, chest still uncovered.

Tyler made a production of settling back down to watch the movie, but within moments, Hearn felt his lover's warm hand inch its way towards his cock. Grinning, Hearn ran his hand through the silky brown hair lying against his chest. "Not interested in the movie?"

"Huh? Yeah, sure. Just can't find a comfortable position."

"Hmmm." Hearn reached under the blanket and moved Tyler's hand closer to his cock. "That help?"

Tyler began slowly stroking Hearn's shaft. "Yeah, thanks."

"No. Thank you," Hearn groaned, bending one leg out to the side to give Tyler more room to play.

As he stroked his hand up and down the ridges of Tyler's spine, he sighed. He knew this was what he wanted, a simple life with the man he loved. The thought of bringing Gracie into the mix would be icing on the cake, but he needed to do things in the right order. He'd thought of little else since he'd first told Tyler he loved him, but it was too soon. Sure, he'd loved the man for a year, but he'd also been carrying around the guilt of Mitch's death. Somehow he knew he needed to be completely over the ordeal with his ex before asking Tyler to move in.

"You okay?" Tyler asked.

"Yeah."

"You must be doing some heavy duty thinking, because my new toy no longer seems interested in playing."

Hearn chuckled. "Well, maybe you could revive it with a little resuscitation, if you know what I mean?"

Tyler rolled to lie between Hearn's already-spread legs. "I thought you'd never ask," he said, diving under the covers.

Chapter Eight

"Just four left to deliver," Tyler told Hearn, placing the bouquets in a cardboard box for safe travel.

"Five," Hearn informed him. "I need you to make up one for Mitch's grave."

Tyler almost dropped the vase of three dozen roses. "What?" He felt like his heart was being ripped out of his chest. After all that had happened the previous several weeks, Tyler assumed Hearn was over Mitch.

Hearn had the decency to look down at the floor. "It's something I need to do."

All his adult life, Tyler had dreamed of spending a Valentine's Day with the man he loved. Somehow having that man take flowers to someone else didn't quite figure in to that particular dream.

Tyler went from hurt to pissed in seconds. He walked over to the refrigerator and grabbed a handful of daisies. Stepping up to Hearn, he shoved the dripping, dishevelled flowers into his hand. "Don't bother giving Mitch my best."

Spinning on his heel, Tyler lifted the bouquets for delivery and strode out the back door to his car. He secured the box with a seatbelt, and climbed behind the wheel, hoping Hearn would emerge from the building and beg his forgiveness.

Several minutes later, Tyler put the car into gear and headed across town to his first delivery. "Dammit!" he screamed at the top of his lungs.

After dropping off the last of the bouquets, he reached for his cell phone and called Wyn.

"Hello," Palmer Wynfield answered.

"Hey, it's Tyler."

"The flowers Hearn delivered are beautiful. Thank you."

"You're welcome, but you should be thanking Ezra."

Wyn chuckled. "Oh I will. Don't you worry about that."

Despite his mood, Tyler found himself grinning. Wyn had always been able to make him smile. The older man had become a pseudo-surrogate father to him.

"Did I catch you at a bad time?" he asked. Wyn had so many irons in the fire lately they hadn't had a chance to get together in over a month.

"Nope. I'm at The Grizzly Bar, having a drink and sitting beside the fire. Care to join me?"

Tyler thought of the drive up the mountain. He normally didn't take his little car on such treacherous roads, but it had been over a week since their last snowfall. "I'll be there in about fifteen minutes."

"Sounds good. Want me to order you something to eat?" Wyn asked.

With his stomach in knots, Tyler knew there was no way he could eat. "No thanks."

"Okay, drive careful."

"Always." Tyler disconnected the phone and turned it off. He thought of turning it back on in case Hearn called, before deciding against it. *Fuck him.* If Hearn needed something he could ask his ex-partner for it, oh yeah, right, he couldn't. Mitch was fucking dead!

* * * *

With the dripping bouquet in his hand, Hearn watched as Tyler stormed out of the store. "Shit."

He tossed the flowers onto the counter and buried his face in his hands. The brass bell over the door rang, signalling someone's arrival. "Tyler stepped out," he barked, trying to get his emotions under control.

"Will he be back?" a deep voice asked.

Turning around, Hearn saw Gill standing there with a big box in his hands. "I'm not sure. He's pissed at me," Hearn offered with a shrug.

Gill walked over and set the box on the counter. "Kyle sent over some leftover pastries." The huge man started to leave, but stopped with his hand on the doorknob. "You okay?"

Hearn shook his head. "I fucked up," he admitted.

Gill chuckled, the sound so deep it rattled Hearn's chest. "Well of course you did. You're a man. We all fuck up from time to time."

Hearn shook his head. "No, I think this was a really bad fuck up."

After glancing at his watch, Gill motioned for Hearn. "Come on. I'll buy you a beer at O'Brien's."

Hearn took one last glance at the flowers on the counter and nodded. He used the spare key to lock the door before following Gill down the street to what used to be Brewster's.

Instead of sitting at the bar, Gill led him to a booth. "Two of the dark brew," Gill called to Sean, before turning back to Hearn. "Okay. It's Valentine's Day. Don't tell me you forgot to give Tyler something."

Hearn shook his head. "I actually had a pretty romantic night set up."

"So what's the problem?" Gill thanked Sean with a nod, as the pub owner set down their drinks.

How did Hearn even begin to explain the way his mind worked? "I planned to ask Tyler to move in with me."

"Sounds good so far."

Hearn took a drink of his beer, licking the foam from his upper lip. "I got this crazy idea that I needed to say goodbye to Mitch before starting my life with Tyler, so I made the mistake of telling the man I love to fix me up a bouquet for Mitch's grave."

"Are you fucking nuts?" Gill asked, nostrils flaring and voice getting loud.

Remembering the hurt expression on Tyler's face, Hearn nodded. "Yeah. I guess I am. It was gonna be my last trip to Mitch's grave."

Gill shook his head and finished off his beer. "I'm no Romeo, and Lord knows I've made stupid mistakes, but damn." Gill, shook his head. He pulled out his phone and handed it to Hearn. "Call him."

Squirming in his seat, Hearn studied the phone in his hand. "But what do I say?"

"Tell him you're an asshole. Tell him you can't live without him." Gill threw up his hands. "Fuck if I know. Whatever it takes."

When his call went straight to voice mail he rolled his eyes and left a short message for Tyler to call him. He pressed the end key and tried to give the phone back to Gill.

The big man crossed his arms and refused to take it. "Don't wimp out now."

What the hell? "It's turned off. What else am I supposed to do?"

Gill uncrossed his arms and leaned across the table. "You know him better than almost anyone. Where would he go to lick his wounds?"

Wyn. He knew how close Tyler was to the older man. Before Wyn had gotten together with Ezra, Hearn had actually been jealous of the men's close relationship. "Wyn, but I don't know his number."

Gill grabbed the phone out of his hand and punched in Wyn's number before handing it back.

It rang three times before Wyn's smooth voice answered. "Hello?"

"It's Hearn."

"I've been expecting your call." Hearn could hear the smile in the older man's voice.

Hearn's throat suddenly felt dry. "You have?"

"Yes."

"Is he with you?" Hearn heard several voices shouting in the background. It was obvious Wyn was either having a party or at his bar.

"Yes."

"Is he still mad?" He held his breath, waiting for the answer.

"You could say that," Wyn replied.

Hearn heard Tyler's voice in the background. "Who's that?" Tyler asked. "If it's Hearn tell him to go fuck himself."

Hearn didn't miss the slurred speech. "Is he drunk?" he asked Wyn.

"You could say that," Wyn repeated.

"I'm on my way. Don't let him drive down the mountain." Hearn hung up before Wyn had a chance to answer. "He's at The Grizzly Bar," he told Gill.

"Well, what're you waiting for? Go kiss his ass."

Hearn grinned at the former professional football player. "You may talk tough, but you're a true romantic underneath all the muscles."

Gill smiled and put his fingers to his lips. "Don't tell anyone. I'll deny it all in a heartbeat."

Within minutes, Hearn was in his truck heading out of town. A huge sign in front of The Gym caught his attention. Slowing the truck to a crawl, he read the bright red letters. "Nate Gills for Mayor."

"Fuck!" He didn't stand a chance.

* * * *

As Nate applied the finishing touches to his present, he thought of DC. Not the meeting with Joseph, though that had gone well, no, he remembered what happened afterward. He'd barely gotten back to the room when Rio had pounced.

For the next four hours, Rio fucked and sucked him in every position imaginable. At one point they'd even called Ryan to include him in on the fun. Hearing his lover's heavy breathing over the speaker phone as Rio rode his ass had been hotter than hell. With a final swish of his brush, Nate also remembered the long plane ride home on an ass so sore he could barely sit.

Setting his supplies aside, he lay down and waited for his men to finish their chores.

By the time Rio and Ryan walked through the back door, Nate had started getting sleepy. "I'm in here," he shouted.

He grinned as his lovers came stumbling into the room, wrestling like a couple of kids. One glance at Nate and they stopped. Rio's jaw was the first to drop, quickly followed by Ryan's.

"Instead of just buying you both a box of chocolates, I decided to do something a little different," Nate explained, glancing down at his nude body covered in painted-on chocolate. "Anyone want a sample before dinner?"

With their tongues hanging out, his men quickly shed their clothing. Lying on a blanket in front of the big stone fireplace, Nate perused his partners. Rio won for speediest erection, but Ryan had him beat in the drool category.

Nate laughed as a drop of saliva actually dripped onto Ryan's tattooed chest. "You gonna waste all that or put it to good use?" To further excite Ryan and Rio, Nate spread his legs in invitation. Damn, he was glad he'd gotten that full wax job while in DC. He couldn't imagine how much scraping the chocolate out of pubes would hurt.

Ryan fell to his knees between Nate's spread thighs. He gently ran a finger over one of Nate's balls. "They look like two big chocolate-covered cherries," Ryan said to Rio.

Rio licked his lips and knelt beside Nate's torso. "Save one for me," he told Ryan, licking a path up the centre of Nate's chest. Sitting back on his heels, he pointed towards Nate. "That's the dividing line. Everything on that half is yours," he informed Ryan, who was busy licking his way around the 'chocolate-covered cherry'.

Nate giggled and shook his head. "How're you gonna divide my hole? I've only got one of 'em."

Rio's eyes rounded as his black brows rose. "Fuck." Rio tapped Ryan on the shoulder. "First one to finish gets his ass."

Ryan waved Rio off without even coming up for air. As Rio hurriedly licked away the chocolate on Nate's stomach and chest, Ryan continued his slow assault below Nate's waist. Ryan appeared more concerned with taking his time than racing towards the finish. The dual sensations were more than enough to keep Nate on edge. He briefly wondered what his men would say if he let go and added a little cream to their dessert.

Rio finished with everything on Nate's upper body, slowing a bit when he licked the confection from Nate's nipple, bucking when his lover sank his teeth into the sensitive flesh.

For the first time since he'd begun, Ryan lifted his head from Nate's groin. "If you want a piece of this cock you'd better get the hell down here."

Rio pulled his mouth from Nate's nipple with a pop. "You tasty motherfucker," Rio growled, thrusting his tongue down Nate's throat.

Nate sighed as Rio broke the kiss and joined Ryan. He was concentrating so hard on not coming, he almost missed the little scuffle between his legs. Opening his eyes, Nate peered down the length of his body to the two men trying to elbow the other out of the way. "Is there a problem?" Nate asked.

"Yeah. We've licked the sides, but Ryan claims it's only fair that he get the head."

"Seriously?" Nate rolled his eyes. "And you call me a baby," he mumbled. He hooked his arms under his knee and rolled to his side, presenting his chocolate-slathered hole. "Better?"

Rio looked at Nate's ass like a starving man. "You got lube? Cuz once I eat it I'm gonna fuck it," Rio growled in his best caveman imitation.

Laughing around the ache in his balls, Nate tossed the lube to Rio. "Have at it," he squeaked, as Ryan's hot mouth engulfed his cock. Nate leaned up on his elbow to watch the carnal scene. "Ohhhh," he moaned as the first lick swept across his ass.

Ryan pumped away at Nate's cock like he was expecting a chocolate fountain to shoot out the end. "Gonna come," he warned, as Rio's tongue dug its way inside his hole.

"Mmmhmm," Ryan moaned, Nate's cock buried in his throat.

Nate's hips bucked towards Ryan's face as he emptied his balls. Ryan started to gag at the force of Nate's stream, but was able to pull off enough to swallow every drop. Nate's head dropped back to the pillow as his eyes rolled to the back of his head. "Fuck." He panted, trying to get his breathing under control, as Rio fucked into him with three fingers.

He managed to open his eyes, when a tongue stroked across his lips. Nate smiled at Ryan. "Thank you," he managed to get out, as Rio drove his cock in deep.

Reaching down, he encircled Ryan's cock in his hand. Ryan moaned and thrust his cum-covered tongue into Nate's willing mouth. As Rio continued to rut in and out of Nate's body, Ryan consumed him with a kiss.

Plastered against Nate's back, Rio's hand joined in pleasuring Ryan's cock. It didn't take long for Rio's roar of pleasure to set Ryan off. Groaning into the kiss, Ryan covered Nate's hand with jets of sticky warmth, as Rio filled Nate's ass.

With both his men panting on either side of him, Nate grinned. *Damn, I give the best gifts.*

* * * *

By the time Hearn entered the bar, it appeared Tyler was on his way to getting majorly shitfaced. He walked over and knelt beside his lover's chair. "Can I talk to you?"

Tyler scowled and gave Wyn the stink eye. "You call him?"

Wyn shook his head. "Hearn was worried about you." Wyn leaned close to Tyler's ear but whispered loud enough for Hearn to hear. "He loves you."

Tyler's gaze shot to Hearn. "I know, dammit. Why do you think I'm sitting here getting drunk off my ass," Tyler pouted.

Hearn held out his hand. "I was able to get a room. Would you at least talk to me?"

He watched as Tyler shifted in his seat before finally standing. Tyler turned to Wyn and gave him a kiss on the cheek. "Thank you. I hope Ezra doesn't get too sore that you had to baby-sit?"

Wyn smiled. "For me, every day is Valentine's Day. Play your cards right and it'll be the same for you."

Hearn shook Wyn's hand before leading a swaying Tyler out of the bar. "Second floor," Hearn said. "Do we need to take the elevator, or can you handle the stairs?"

Tyler rolled his eyes. "I'm not that drunk."

Yeah, you are, Hearn told himself but let it go. With their height difference, he couldn't get a good grip on Tyler's waist. Instead, he hooked his thumb through Tyler's belt loop and helped to hold his lover up.

Tyler stumbled halfway up the grand staircase, but Hearn's hold kept him from toppling down. Tyler regained his balance and slapped at Hearn's hand. "You're givin' me a wedgie."

Chuckling, Hearn relaxed his hold. Digging into his back pocket, he pulled out the key-card and motioned to the right. "Two-fourteen."

Once inside the room, Hearn adjusted the heat as Tyler dropped onto the king-sized bed. As much as Hearn wanted to join his lover, he knew he had a great deal of making up for first.

Sitting on the edge of the mattress, he turned to face Tyler. "I need to explain myself."

"You bet you do," Tyler mumbled.

Hearn reached out and ran his hand over Tyler's shin. "I don't think you have any idea just how much I love you."

Tyler rolled his head to look at Hearn. "You have an odd way of showing it."

"Maybe." Hearn ran his free hand through his hair. "This isn't the way I hoped this night would turn out."

Tyler leaned up on his elbows. "Kinda hard for it to turn out any other way when you decide to take your ex-lover flowers on Valentine's Day," Tyler quipped.

"It was supposed to be the last. I was gonna ask you to move in, but I knew I had to purge myself of any guilt before moving onto the next chapter in my life." Hearn stood and started pacing back and forth over the new carpet. "I fucked up. I know that now."

Before he could say anything more, Tyler bounded off the bed and threw himself into Hearn's arms. "What did you say?" Tyler asked, climbing up Hearn's body to wrap his legs around Hearn's stomach.

With his hands on Tyler's ass to hold him up, Hearn started to repeat what he'd just said. A brief kiss from Tyler stopped him. "Not that part. I couldn't give a fuck about Mitch. Ask me to move in. Please, ask me?"

The clamp surrounding his heart loosened. "Will you make me the happiest man alive and move in?"

Tyler buried his fingers in Hearn's hair and kissed him, pushing his tongue in deep. The kiss was all the confirmation Hearn needed, as he fell onto the bed with Tyler still in his arms.

Coming up for air, Tyler shook his head. "See? Was that so hard?"

Chuckling, Hearn pulled Tyler's shirt off over his head. "I'll take that as a yes."

Tyler sat up, straddling Hearn's waist. "I've loved you since the day I met you. I know it sounds corny but it's true, and I would like nothing more than to shack up with you."

Hearn reached up and ran his fingertips over Tyler's chest, paying particular attention to the brown pebbled nipples. "There's something else I want to talk to you about." He hoped he already knew Tyler's answer, but as the day had already shown him, he didn't always get things right. "I want us to petition for guardianship of Gracie."

Tyler's brows shot to his dishevelled bangs. "You mean adopt her?"

Hearn nodded. "If they'll let us."

Tyler's face seemed to take on a faraway expression. "It's a big responsibility raising a child. We haven't even talked about the important issues involved."

"Like?"

Crossing his arms, Tyler's entire body seemed to tense. "I won't spank her. Ever."

"Discipline is an important part of parenting. We may not always like it, but we can't allow Gracie to run the house either."

Tyler shook his head. "I'm not talking about discipline. I get she'll probably need to be grounded or whatever else we come up with, but I need your word that you'll never touch her in anger."

Noticing the rigid set of Tyler's jaw, a light suddenly went off in Hearn's head. Tyler's inability earlier to stand and confront Hearn when he'd hurt him. The vomiting at Hearn's anger the first night they declared their love...it all made sense. Pulling Tyler down against him, Hearn buried his face in his lover's hair. "Who hurt you, baby? Was it your parents?"

Tyler's breath hitched as the muscles under Hearn's hands relaxed. Tyler pressed himself even closer to Hearn. "Just Dad. Not all the time. Only when I tried to get him to stop beating on Mom."

Hearing the pain in his lover's voice, Hearn began peppering kisses to Tyler's temple, slowly moving to his lips. "I'm not your dad." As he gave in to Tyler's need for a deeper kiss, he tried to imagine what it must have been like for Tyler as a child. He wondered if Tyler had ever sought treatment.

Breaking the kiss, he looked into Tyler's sad brown eyes. "I'll never raise a hand to you. You know that, right?"

Tyler nodded.

"But you have to deal with the fact that there'll be arguments. We won't always see eye to eye."

"I know."

Rolling them over, so he was on top, Hearn met Tyler's gaze once again. "Don't be afraid to argue back. Sometimes I need a swift kick in the ass to make me see reason."

Tyler grinned. "Like earlier?"

"Yeah, like earlier." Hearn reached between them and unfastened Tyler's jeans. "Can we get to the makeup sex now? That's the best part of arguing."

Chapter Nine

Hearn threw his pencil onto the coffee table and rubbed his eyes. "I need to just pull out of the race. No way in hell I can win against Nate anyway."

Tyler set down his glass of wine and crawled into Hearn's lap. "You only have three weeks left."

Hearn readjusted Tyler so he was straddling his lap. "Do you honestly think I can win?"

Gazing into Hearn's deep brown eyes, he knew he couldn't lie. "No. I don't." Before Hearn could say anything more, Tyler put his finger to his lover's lips, silencing him. "But this is about more than winning. It's about getting your ideas for the park system out to the townspeople."

Hearn nodded. "I know, but I can't help thinking I'm spending too much time giving speeches and interviews. I should be focussing on you and Gracie." Hearn pointed to the opposite side of the house. "Helping you get her room ready. Not sitting here trying to figure out how to fix the town's budget concerns."

Tyler leaned forward and nipped Hearn's lower lip. "We still have four days until the temporary guardianship goes before the judge. That should be plenty of time for you to help me put the finishing touches on the princess's castle."

Hearn smiled, pulling Tyler in for a kiss. "Have I told you how spectacular that room is, by the way? Gracie's gonna flip when she sees it."

Feeling good about what he'd managed to accomplish, Tyler preened under the compliment. "Scary how much I want to move myself into that room," he laughed.

Hearn laughed along with him. "Maybe someday we can sneak one of the pretty little boas out for you to play with."

Tyler slapped Hearn's chest. "Don't be ridiculous." He purposely waited a beat before adding. "I've already got one in red."

Laughing so hard he had to hold his side, Hearn shook his head. "See? This is a lot more fun than looking at boring numbers."

"I agree, but come summer you're gonna want these programmes in place. If you truly want to present the plan, you'll have to figure out how to pay for it. Otherwise they won't take you seriously." Tyler gave Hearn one more kiss before climbing off. "Now, I'm gonna watch my TV show and you're gonna get back to work."

He started to settle back in against his corner of the couch, but a heavy-lidded look from Hearn changed his mind. "I'll just sit over here," he excused himself, sitting in the chair beside the fireplace.

* * * *

Nate watched Hearn put a stack of papers back into an envelope. The town meeting had gone well, and Hearn had impressed the hell out of him.

"You ready?" Ryan asked, interrupting his train of thought.

"In a minute. I wanna talk to Hearn first." Nate turned to give Ryan a kiss before walking over to Hearn.

"Very well done," he congratulated, shaking Hearn's hand.

"Thanks," Hearn replied, gazing down at the floor. "I'm not much on public speaking, but you probably figured that out."

Nate smiled. Despite what Hearn said, Nate had witnessed a change in the man over the previous month and a half. The Hearn Sutherland he knew a year ago would have never had the self-confidence to run for mayor. "I liked what you had to say." He slapped Hearn on the shoulder. "Delivery and all."

"I know I can't beat you, but I'd already entered the race before I found out you were running as well." Hearn glanced up and out to the milling crowd.

Nate could tell the moment Hearn spotted Tyler. Hearn's love was almost as palpable as he stared at his lover. "I wanted to quit, ya know, but Tyler reminded me of something I taught our soon-to-be daughter."

"And what's that?" Nate asked.

"Nothing wrong with losing. It's willing to play in the first place that's important," Hearn recited, as Tyler walked up to wrap his arms around him.

"That's right," Tyler agreed, giving Hearn a kiss.

"I hear congratulations are in order," Nate said, shaking Tyler's hand.

At Tyler's questioning expression, Nate continued. "Hearn told me you're adopting?"

Tyler's entire face lit up. "Yep. A six-year-old little girl named Gracie." Tyler became animated when he began bragging about the girl. "Wait 'til you meet her. She's the cutest kid I've ever seen and will have you wrapped around her finger in no time."

Nate smiled, Tyler's happiness was infectious. "You'll have to be sure and bring her by the house. I'd love to see her with Rio and Ryan."

"What woman are you trying to push on us now?" Ryan asked, stepping up beside Nate.

"Gracie," Nate informed him. "She's the little girl Hearn and Tyler are adopting."

"Fantastic." Ryan reached out to shake the new parents' hands.

"You guys ever think about it? There are plenty of kids at the centre in need of a good home," Hearn offered.

Ryan chuckled and shook his head. He wrapped his arm around Nate's head and rubbed his scalp with his knuckles. "It's all Rio and I can do to keep up with the kid we've got."

Nate slapped Ryan's hands away. "Ryan, the hair." Nate ran his fingers through his hair, repairing the damage his lover had done.

"See what I mean?" Ryan asked, grinning.

"Yo," Rio's voice called across the room. "You guys about ready?"

Nate waved to his gorgeous hunk beside the door. "Sorry, Rio's hot to get home before he misses his show." He leaned forward. "Desperate Housewives," he said in a loud stage-whisper.

Hearn and Tyler started laughing. "Come on lover, take me home," Nate chuckled, taking Ryan's hand. "Make sure you come by after Gracie gets settled in."

"We will," Hearn replied.

Ryan put his arm around Nate as they neared Rio. "Have you ever seen Hearn so happy?"

"No," Ryan agreed, pulling Nate closer to his side. "It looks good on him."

"Sure as hell does."

"Come on," Rio whined. "I've already pulled the truck up."

Nate chuckled and rolled his eyes. "We're coming."

He let his men lead him outside. Like usual, Nate sat in the centre between Ryan and Rio. "I liked Hearn's ideas for the after-school and summer kids' programmes."

Ryan nodded his agreement. "He's definitely done his homework as far as finding the money in the town's budget. And I think he's right about making community service hours mandatory for high school graduates. They'll not only learn to become more civic minded, but it'll look good on their college resumes."

Nate went quiet. Maybe Hearn would be better at the job as mayor. He'd definitely shown the town his superior business skills earlier in the evening. Nate didn't want to admit it, but he knew he'd win the election. Hearn was a nice guy, but he rarely talked with people outside of the park.

He felt a hand slide up his thigh to rub against his cock. Nate glanced sideways at Ryan. "Yes?"

"What's got you thinking so hard?"

Nate shrugged. "If Hearn would make a better mayor."

Ryan's arm dipped from the back of his seat to Nate's shoulders, pulling him closer. "I think Hearn is a wonderful man. Lord knows he's a hell of a lot smarter than that jackass Mitch ever gave him credit for, but no. I don't think he'd make a better town leader."

"But you just said…"

"I know what I said, but you have to possess a certain amount of finesse to do the job justice. You, my dear, have that in spades. People listen to you because they want to, not because they have to. Do you see the difference?"

Nate grinned. "Because I'm the cutest guy in school I might get to wear the homecoming crown?"

Both Rio and Ryan burst out laughing. "Yeah, something like that," Ryan chuckled, with a shake to his head.

* * * *

Tyler ran his hand down Hearn's bare chest. "I'm so proud of you."

Hearn reached down and covered Tyler's hand, bringing it up to his mouth for a kiss. "Thanks. I was actually quite pleased with the presentation. I may not win the election, but at least I got people thinking."

"Exactly," Tyler agreed. Tyler sat up on his knees and studied Hearn. "You don't really want to be Mayor Sutherland anyway, do you?"

"No, not really," Hearn admitted. He still hadn't divulged to Tyler the real reason he'd decided to run. Maybe it was time he laid his cards out on the table. "I did it to make you proud of me."

Tyler leaned over, putting a hand on either side of Hearn's head. With his face two inches from Hearn's, Tyler's eyes narrowed. "What're you talking about?"

With Tyler in his face, Hearn couldn't back away enough to avoid eye contact. "I know it was a stupid thing to do, but at the time I didn't think I was worthy of someone like you."

Tyler stuck his tongue out and rimmed Hearn's lips. "Does this go back to the way Mitch made you feel?"

"Yeah. Everyone in town likes you, and you do a hell of a lot for them in return. I thought if I showed you I cared about Cattle Valley as much as you seem to...well, that you'd think I was good enough."

"Good enough for what? I'd already told you I loved you."

"That's not always enough," Hearn confessed. *It sure as hell wasn't for Mitch.* That is, if Mitch ever loved him in the first place. *No.* Hearn had to believe his ex felt something.

Tyler sat up and crossed his arms. "I have a feeling this insecurity goes beyond Mitch." Tyler reached down and cupped Hearn's face. "Did you get along with your parents before they found out you were gay?"

What? Hearn felt like he'd been slapped. *Where was this coming from?* "They were adults."

"So?"

Hearn shrugged. "So? They weren't around much. They were wealthy. They had better things to do."

Tyler bent down and kissed him. "Did they love you?"

"I don't know, I guess. Hell, they were my parents. I had the best of everything growing up, the best schools, the best nannies, the biggest toys." Hearn didn't want to talk about his past. He ran his hands down Tyler's back to his ass. Spreading his lover's cheeks, he circled the puckered hole with his middle finger.

Tyler moaned, before shaking his head. "Stop trying to distract me," he scolded.

"I don't wanna talk about my parents."

"Why?"

Exasperated, Hearn sighed. "Because they don't mean anything to me! Surely, you of all people can understand that. I've talked to my mother a few times on the phone, but it's not like she'd ever ask me to visit."

"Why wouldn't she ask you to visit? Goddammit, Hearn, she's your mother."

Hearn shook his head. "Just forget it. I don't need someone with a fucked-up childhood trying to psychoanalyse mine."

Tyler stared at him for a few moments before jumping off the bed. Hearn watched his partner's back visibly stiffen as he walked towards the bathroom. The door slammed and Hearn groaned. "Fuck!"

He was just about to go after Tyler, when the door swung open with such force it made a small dent in the wall behind it. With fire in his eyes, Tyler marched back over to the bed.

"Let me tell you something," Tyler began, finger pointing at Hearn in anger. "My 'childhood' may have been fucked up, but at least my mom told me that she loved me, every goddamned day. Which is more than I think you can say. I think you clung to that piece of shit, Mitch, because he was the first person to show you an ounce of caring."

Hearn rose from his position until he was eye level with the man having a tantrum right in front of him. He held up a hand in warning. "Put the finger away," he growled.

Tyler froze. Hearn watched as his lover's gaze went to his outstretched hand and the finger in question. He saw the reaction in Tyler's eyes first. The outstretched hand came in to cover Tyler's mouth as he turned to retreat to the bathroom.

Jumping out of bed, Hearn quickly followed. "Breathe, baby," he instructed from the doorway. "Just relax and concentrate."

Tyler shook his head, falling onto his knees in front of the toilet. "I'm sorry," Tyler stuttered, lifting the lid.

"Don't be," Hearn warned. "It's the first time you've probably ever stood up for yourself."

Tyler closed his eyes and rested his forehead on the arms braced across the cold porcelain. Hearn watched as Tyler took several deep breaths. "Easy," Hearn soothed, sliding in to sit behind the man he loved.

"I shouldn't have said those things to you," Tyler choked around a sob.

Hearn rested his cheek against Tyler's back, needing the connection. "I'm glad you did." He teased the hair at the nape of Tyler's neck. "You were probably right. When I found Mitch, I thought...at last."

It hurt to admit it, even to himself, but he'd needed Mitch's love so much he'd turned a blind eye to everything. "I think he probably fucked around our entire relationship. Maybe that's why I didn't notice a difference once we moved to Cattle Valley." Hearn shrugged. "I didn't want to see it. I finally had someone who, at least on the surface, seemed to put me first."

Tyler pressed back. "Hold me?"

Hearn sat up and gathered Tyler into his lap, and wiped his lover's tears.

"I love you," Tyler declared, chin wobbling.

Tilting Tyler's face up, Hearn kissed him. As he tasted the interior of Tyler's mouth he thanked God he'd been given such a special gift. He knew the addition of Gracie would be a welcome one, but he also knew he'd have felt complete even if it were just him and Tyler for the rest of their lives. "I love you, too."

"Take me to bed."

Getting his feet under him, Hearn scooped Tyler up from the floor and carried him out of the bathroom, laying him gently on the mattress. He tossed the lube they'd used earlier onto the bed before coming down on top of his lover. He truly was proud of Tyler for standing up for himself. Although arguing wasn't something he looked forward to, it was important for Tyler to understand he could speak his mind.

He began kissing his way up Tyler's neck, taking the time to cherish what he had. Reaching Tyler's mouth, he brushed his lips over Tyler's. With a moan, Tyler opened for him, begging with unspoken words.

As he finally kissed his lover, he reached for the tube beside the pillow. He slicked his cock and guided it to Tyler's already stretched hole.

"Make love to me," Tyler whispered against Hearn's lips.

"Every day in every way," Hearn answered, slowly pushing his way inside Tyler's heat.

Even as his hips began to move, Hearn knew this was more than making love. It was a cementing of their bond. Tyler's body moulded to Hearn's, moving with him on every thrust.

Riding the edge of his climax, Hearn realised he'd never truly made love. Even though he'd been sexually active for quite a few years, he'd always equated a slow fuck as making love. How wrong he'd been. Gazing into Tyler's eyes, Hearn felt as much with his heart as he did his dick. The pleasure wasn't simply physical, but spiritual as well. *Yeah. That's the difference*, he concluded as he spilled his seed deep inside the man he loved.

Chapter Ten

"The Gym," Rio answered the phone.

"Hi, Rio. It's Joseph. Is Will there by chance?"

"*Nate's* making last minute preparations for the party later. Did something happen?" They'd managed to keep Nate's birth name out of the papers, but that didn't mean the Senator hadn't found out.

"Nate, yes, I'm sorry. I forgot it was Election Day for you guys. Tell me, how're his chances?"

"Good. As a matter of fact, we're combining parties with the other candidate."

"Really?"

Rio chuckled. "Yeah, you gotta know Cattle Valley. When the guy you're running against is a friend, it's all pretty civilised."

"I've got to get out there someday and see this Utopia first hand."

"You should. We'd love to have you, provided you bring Phillip along," Rio teased.

Joseph chuckled. "I promise to never try and poach Nate."

"Good to know."

"Listen, I had something I wanted to run past Nate, but since I have you on the phone, do you mind if I ask you a question?"

"Okay, shoot." Rio peered around the room, making sure no one needed his assistance.

"I was wondering what the job situation is like in Cattle Valley? You see, I've got a kid who just turned eighteen and is no longer eligible for the programme. Problem is, he really has nowhere else to go."

"Is he trained in any certain vocation?" Rio asked.

"Formally? No. But he's worked in the kitchen here at the shelter since he first wandered through our doors three years ago. He's a damn fine cook, I can vouch for that."

Rio rubbed his chin. "Let me talk to a few people and get back to you. I mean, he's more than welcome to come here without a job, but it might make the transition easier on him if he knows he's moving towards something."

Joseph was silent for a moment. "Yes. He's become quite attached to us over the years. But recently he's been having problems with an ex. Phillip and I think it would be best to get him out of the city before the ex does something more serious than slapping him around."

Rio gripped the phone. There was nothing he hated more than to hear about abuse of any kind. "Put him on the next plane. If I can't find him something, I'll give him a job here at the gym."

"Thanks," Joseph sighed. "You don't know what a relief that is."

"Do you want me to wire you some money for a plane ticket?"

"No. We'll dip into some of the money Nate sent if you think that would be okay with him?"

"It'll be fine. Nate donated that money for you and Phillip to use as you see fit. It sounds like keeping this kid safe is a good enough reason. By the way, what's his name?"

"Jay De Luca. And, Rio, there's something else I should warn you about."

By the tone of Joseph's voice, Rio wasn't sure he was going to like what his new friend had to say. "What?"

"Jay's...delicate."

The first thing that popped into his head was china. "You mean breakable, or feminine?"

"Both, actually." Joseph paused once again before continuing. "You did tell me Cattle Valley was tolerant, right?"

"Yes. I don't think you need to worry about Jay being flamboyant here. Hell, look at Nate."

Joseph cleared his throat. "Jay isn't flamboyant in the least. He's quite shy, but his mannerisms...well, let's just say they make a lot of people uncomfortable. It's the reason we've let him stay here so long. He wouldn't be safe on the streets, if you know what I mean."

"Don't worry. I'll keep an eye out for him, but I honestly don't foresee any trouble." Rio wondered what he'd gotten himself into. Still, it sounded like Jay needed a safe place to live, and Rio couldn't think of a safer place than Cattle Valley. "Make the arrangements, and give me a call back. I'll make sure he gets picked up from the airport, either by me or someone I trust."

"I can't thank you enough," Joseph replied.

"No need. This is exactly what this town was founded for."

After hanging up, Rio went to find Mario. He had a spare room and job to find.

* * * *

"You two about ready?" Hearn asked, walking into Gracie's room. Tyler was putting the finishing touches on Gracie's hair. "Ready?" he asked again.

Tyler fastened the bow holding Gracie's black curls out of her face. "I think so." Tyler stood and turned their daughter around to face him. "What do you think?"

"Pretty as a picture," Hearn complimented.

Tyler had insisted they buy Gracie a new dress for the election party. Hearn had tried to argue that she already had a closet full of new clothes, but Tyler rolled his eyes and bought one anyway.

"You're going to spoil her," Hearn had admonished.

"Yep," Tyler had agreed. "And she deserves every bit of it."

Leaning against the wall, Hearn looked at the two people he loved most in the world. *They both deserve to be spoiled.* He watched as Tyler lifted Gracie off her bed.

"We're ready," Tyler said, leading Gracie by the hand.

Hearn reached down and picked his daughter up. "You'll steal everyone's heart." He placed a kiss on Gracie's nose, before turning to give Tyler a kiss. "Let's get this over with so we can come home and watch television."

Shaking his head, Tyler led them out to their new SUV. Hearn set Gracie in her booster seat and buckled her up. "All ready, princess?"

"Yes, Daddy."

Shutting the car door, Hearn needed a moment to get his emotions under control. After the judge had granted him Temporary-Guardianship, Gracie had started calling him Daddy and Tyler, Dad. Hearn doubted he'd ever take it for granted. They still had some red tape to wade through before Gracie was officially theirs, but at least they were able to bring the precious little girl home with them.

Opening the driver's door, Hearn climbed behind the wheel. "Let's go do the concession thing and then get the hel...heck out of there."

In a town the size of Cattle Valley it hadn't taken long to count the votes. Hearn had received his call before he'd begun to dress for the party. The election had ended as he knew it would, but he was still rather shocked by how many votes he'd actually received.

Tyler's hand landed on his thigh. "Doesn't matter that you lost. I have a strong feeling you accomplished what you set out to do."

With a nod, Hearn backed out of the drive and headed for the reception hall connected to the church. When he pulled into the parking lot, the party appeared to be in full swing. "Nate does know how to throw a party," Hearn commented.

Tyler chuckled. "That's because Nate *is* the party."

They had barely walked into the hall when Rio came up to them. "Can I talk to you for a minute?" he asked Tyler.

"Sure." He held up a finger and pointed towards Nate. "Gracie, why don't you go give Mayor Gills a big hug and tell him congratulations."

Hearn was actually shocked when Gracie squealed in delight and ran towards Nate. He gave Tyler a questioning expression.

Tyler grinned. "She spent all day with the man decorating for a party, what did you expect?"

Chuckling, Hearn wrapped his arm around Tyler's waist as his partner spoke. "Okay, I'm sorry about that."

Rio smiled. "No big deal. Nate's crazy about her."

"Well he can't have her," Hearn added.

Rio shifted a little and glanced over towards the back wall. "I was wondering if you'd rented your loft out yet?"

Tyler's head tilted to the side. "No. Why?"

"I thought maybe you'd lease it to me. I just picked Cattle Valley's newest resident up from the airport." Rio gestured to the young woman standing in the corner.

"You mean that girl over there?" Tyler asked.

Rio rubbed the back of his neck. "*His* name's Jay De Luca. It's a long story which I'll be more than happy to fill you in on later, but for now, he needs a place to stay. I've also promised to help him find a job."

Hearn gazed at the tiniest, thinnest, *hell*, prettiest man he'd ever set eyes on. No way was that a man. "Really? That's a guy?" he couldn't keep from asking.

Rio nodded. "He's barely spoken two words since I picked him up. Don't know that I've ever met anyone so quiet. You shouldn't have a bit of trouble from him if you decide to let him live above the store," Rio told Tyler.

Tyler waved away Rio's concerns. "He looks so sad and lonely," Tyler whispered.

Hearn bent and kissed Tyler's temple. "Go on. I know you want to."

Tyler gazed up at Hearn. "You're sure you don't mind if I go over and introduce myself?"

"You wouldn't be you if you didn't try and take care of the world." Hearn gave his lover a kiss. "Go. I'll catch up with you in a bit."

As Tyler made his way through the crowd, Hearn looked for Gracie. "It appears as though Gracie's weaving her magic," he chuckled.

Rio followed Hearn's gaze and shook his head. "Damn," he huffed. "No matter what they say, we are not adopting a child. One princess in the house is enough." Rio started across the hall with Hearn on his heels.

Gracie did indeed look like a princess sitting on the throne of Ryan's arm. Hearn couldn't hear what she was talking about, but her gestures were dramatic. Nate and Ryan were in stitches by the time Hearn and Rio approached.

"What're you telling these men, Gracie?"

Gracie immediately reached for Hearn. He easily took his princess in his arms and hugged her. At six, Gracie might be too old to hold like this, but with her small body-size, she fit Hearn's arms perfectly.

"I was telling Sheriff Blackfeather and Mayor Gills about my tea set. They said they'd come over sometime."

Rio made a sound in his throat and rolled his eyes. "I'll be sure and drop them off before I go play pool or something."

Hearn laughed. As tough as Rio wanted everyone to think he was, Hearn knew the man was a marshmallow underneath. Gracie would be having tea for four before he knew it.

Balancing Gracie on one arm, Hearn stuck his hand out to Nate. "Congratulations, Mayor."

Nate smiled and returned the handshake. "Thanks. I've got a few things I'd like to discuss with you when you get a moment."

"Oh?"

Nate nodded, but before he could say anything more, George Manning stepped up to shake his hand. Hearn politely excused himself and carried Gracie over to the food table. "You hungry?"

Gracie studied the table of food. "Do I gotta eat veggies?" she asked, scrunching up her nose.

"Nope, not this time." He set her down on the floor and picked up two plates. "You point to what you want," he told her, as he moved down the buffet.

After setting their plates on an empty table, Hearn went back for two glasses of punch. "Now don't spill it on your pretty dress," he warned.

"I'm not a baby," she informed him.

Hearn leaned over and kissed her. "Yes you are. You're *my* baby."

"Ooh, yummy, dinner," Tyler joked, kissing Gracie's neck.

Giggling, Gracie pushed Tyler away. "My neck is not your snack. Get your own."

Instead of going to the food table, Tyler took a seat on Hearn's lap and stole one of his chicken wings. "Hearn'll share with me."

Hearn's hand landed squarely on Tyler's hip. "Get your own, moocher."

In a mock pout, Tyler stood and headed for the buffet. Hearn leaned over towards Gracie. "I would've given him more if he would've asked nicely."

Gracie was still giggling when Tyler returned to the table, plate loaded. "So what did you think of your new tenant?" Hearn asked, biting into a stuffed mushroom.

Tyler paused with a carrot stick half-way to his mouth. "There's something about his voice. I can't describe it. He doesn't talk much, but when he does, it's...hypnotic."

Hearn finished off his mushroom. "How so?"

Tyler shook his head. "I don't know, soft, serene. The kind of voice you'd expect an angel to have." Tyler shook his head. "I told you I wouldn't be able to describe it."

Tyler gazed across the room at where Jay was sitting. "I tried to get him to join us, but he said he felt better staying out of the way." Tyler put his hand to his chest. "If he were a few years younger I think I'd adopt him myself."

Hearn glanced at the young man. Telling himself he had nothing to be jealous of, he glanced back at Tyler. "I don't need to worry about the two of you, do I?"

Tyler lobbed the carrot stick at him. "Don't be a dork. I guess he just brings out my maternal instincts or something. Anyway, don't judge me until after you've met him."

"Whatever," Hearn quipped, throwing the carrot back at Tyler.

Hearn took a bite of his brownie when a chicken wing hit him in the face. Startled, he swallowed the bite before he could get it chewed. The large piece of food started to get stuck in his throat, he gasped for a breath and grabbed his glass of punch, trying like hell to soften the brownie. After a bit of coughing, he was finally able to get a breath. He glanced down at the wing on the table and turned to Gracie. "Did you just throw that at me?"

Gracie clapped her hands and giggled. "I wanted to play like you and Dad," she informed him.

Hearn scowled at Tyler who was cracking up. "Nice. Teaching your daughter to throw food."

* * * *

Cleaning up the last of the mess, Rio put the broom away. "You guys about ready to hit it?"

"Yeah," Nate yawned. "Just let me finish wrapping these leftovers. I'll take 'em home for now. Thought maybe I'd give them to Jay in the morning. I doubt Tyler left anything in his kitchen to eat."

"Want me to start loading them up?"

"Sure," Nate yawned again.

Rio grabbed a big box full of food. He peered over his shoulder at Ryan. "You gonna just stand there? Can't you see your boss needs to get to bed?" Rio chuckled on his way out to Nate's SUV. He knew Ryan hadn't given the small detail much thought, but officially, as soon as Nate was sworn in, he'd become Ryan's boss. "God, is this a great country or what?"

He put the box in the back of the vehicle and went back in for the next load. He wasn't sure how many people Nate had expected to feed, but they had a ton of leftovers. Jay would be eating high on the hog for days. Not that the skinny fella couldn't use it. Damn, he'd never seen anyone as tiny as Jay. Although the guy was probably five-foot-six or seven, Rio bet Jay didn't weigh more than a hundred and five or ten pounds.

Ryan stumbled out as Rio was going in. "Is your boss about ready?" Rio asked, twisting the knife.

"Shut up," Ryan snarled.

"Or what?" Rio taunted.

"Or I'll sell my third of The Gym to Nate and he'll become your boss, too."

"Damn. You fight dirty," Rio said, pretending to lock his lips and throw away the key.

Nate met Rio at the door and handed him another box. "That's the last one. I'll lock up."

Rio loaded the food into the SUV and got behind the wheel. Thankfully, he'd taken Jay over to the loft earlier, because all he wanted was to get home and crawl into bed. It had been a big day for all of them, especially their new mayor.

Instead of fighting over who would ride shotgun, Nate opened the back door and climbed in. "Wake me when we get home," he mumbled.

Ryan got in the passenger seat and buckled up. "I'm damn proud of you, Nate," He reached over the back of the seat to swat Nate's ass.

Nate was already so out of it, he didn't even protest, simply grunted a reply neither of them could understand. Chuckling, Rio pulled out of the parking lot. "I wonder how big his head'll get once all this sinks in?" he mused.

"Shit, if I know Nate, the only thing that'll change is we'll have to go to City Hall to satisfy his mid-day hungers," Ryan joked.

"I heard that," Nate piped up from the backseat.

"You denying it?" Rio chimed in.

"Nope."

"Didn't think so," Rio said with a grin.

Epilogue

"It's Sunday, where're you going?" Hearn asked, from his position on the couch.

"To the shop, but I won't be long," Tyler answered. He hated not telling Hearn the entire truth. He'd gone over it a hundred times, and there was something he needed to do.

"Can you stop by and pick up something for dessert? Nate and the guys are coming over for lunch."

Slipping on his light jacket, Tyler gave Hearn a quick kiss. "If you promise not to wake Gracie from her nap, I'll pick up a pie. Although it's Sunday, so Kyle's is closed. You'll have to make do with one from the grocery store."

"Mmm, sounds good. Cherry if you can find one," Hearn's attention returned to the movie.

Tyler drove to the shop and parked in back. He turned up the stereo as he worked, putting together the bouquet. After gathering a rather large bunch of daisies, he started to automatically reach for the roses, but stopped himself. Nope. Roses were too good for this particular arrangement.

With the stems tied with ribbon, Tyler switched off the stereo and locked up. The drive to the cemetery wasn't long, just outside of town. He parked the car, happy to see he was the only person there. What he had to say to Mitch was private.

Flowers in hand, he easily found Mitch's grave. He smiled at the remnants of the last bouquet Hearn had delivered. Picking up the faded and torn ribbon, he stuffed it in his pocket.

Tyler propped the fresh flowers against the headstone and stepped back. "This is it, Mitch. The last bouquet you'll ever get from me or Hearn. He's mine now, mine and Gracie's. You were a fool for not holding on to what you had, but your stupidity gave me a family, and for that I'd like to say thank you."

Tears burned his eyes at the thought of living a life without the man he loved. "He's everything to me, and I make damn sure I let him know that on a daily basis."

Chuckling, he had to do a bit of bragging. "You gave up on him too soon. Even you would've been proud of the man he's become. Although I doubt he'd have had the confidence to take chances if he were still under your constant criticisms. Hearn's now the Parks and Recreation Department Director. He's already started programmes that have made a big difference."

Tyler kicked at a clump of greening grass. "Well, that's about all I have to say to you. Thanks for giving me the best lover and partner a man could ask for, and thanks for giving Gracie the best daddy in the world."

Turning away, Tyler walked back to his car, feeling better than he had in a long time. He'd been meaning to have that little talk with Mitch for a while, but in his life, the living took precedence.

After stopping off at the grocery store, he pulled into the drive, happy to see Rio's pickup already parked there. He lifted the two cherry pies from the passenger seat and went inside. He was a little surprised to see the living room empty, but heard voices coming from Gracie's room. Damn. He wondered which one of her new 'uncles' had woken her from her nap.

Tyler set the dessert boxes on the kitchen island before going to investigate. The door to Gracie's room was open enough for Tyler to peek inside without being noticed. He covered a laugh, as he observed Rio sitting in one of the tiny chairs with a red feather boa around his neck. Gracie was pouring pretend tea and telling her new playmate all about school.

He never thought he'd see the day. Nate had been over several times for Gracie's now-famous tea parties, but Rio had always been adamant about not joining in. Tyler didn't know whether to tease the big guy or not. Rio looked like he was having the time of his life. He thought about running to get his camera to capture the moment.

In the end, he decided it wouldn't be fare. Tyler walked back and quietly opened the door before slamming it. "I'm home. Where is everyone?"

He barely suppressed a laugh when Rio came sauntering out of the bedroom, minus the boa. "Nate, Ryan and Hearn needed to run to City Hall for a minute, so I told 'em I'd keep an eye on Gracie."

"Oh? Is she awake?" Tyler had to turn away when he noticed a red feather caught in Rio's black curls.

"Yep, just now," Rio said, acting more manly than usual.

"Well, if you don't mind watching her a little longer, I'll get lunch started."

"Okay. Just holler if you need me," Rio said, going back into the bedroom.

As Tyler fixed the marinade for the steaks, he finally let out the laugh he'd suppressed for so long. Life was good.

About the Author

An avid reader for years, one day Carol Lynne decided to write her own brand of erotic romance. Carol juggles between being a full-time mother and a full-time writer. These days, you can usually find Carol either cleaning jelly out of the carpet or nestled in her favourite chair writing steamy love scenes.

Carol loves to hear from readers. You can find her contact information, website details and author profile page at http://www.total-e-bound.com

Total-E-Bound Publishing

www.total-e-bound.com

Take a look at our exciting range of literagasmic™
erotic romance titles and discover pure quality
at Total-E-Bound.

Made in the USA